"The battle for the bed starts at noon."

She held out her hand and Sam shook it.

She began to pull away but he slipped his hand around her waist and drew her against his body. His lips covered hers in a deep kiss, their tongues creating a delicious connection that he didn't want to break. When she broke away, he looked down into her wide eyes.

"May the best man win," he whispered.

Her expression hardened and she wrapped her hand around the nape of his neck and pulled him into another kiss. Her mouth was soft and searching, her tongue tracing the width of his mouth, teasing him in a way that was more provocative than he expected, and his whole body reacted.

But Amelia wasn't about to let him take control. She stepped away and gave him a coy smile, her lips still damp and glistening.

"Don't you mean the best woman?"

Dear Reader,

As I was writing this book, my editor, Adrienne Macintosh, mentioned to me that she enjoyed my small-town books. I hadn't realized until that moment how many times I find myself setting a story in a charming, picturesque but quirky small town. I love the eccentric characters I usually find in these imaginary towns and villages.

And how to properly use a small town? Give it a historic inn with a sexy innkeeper. Toss in some colorful townsfolk. Bring on the heroine, a big-city career girl. Add a snowstorm, and we're off to a fun romance!

I hope you enjoy the book as much as I enjoyed writing it.

And next up, the Quinns are back for more adventures!

Happy reading,

Kate Hoffmann

Kate Hoffmann

Compromising Positions

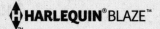

Recycling programs for this product may not exist in your area.

ISBN-13: 978-0-373-79888-9

Compromising Positions

Printed in U.S.A.

Kate Hoffmann lives in southeastern Wisconsin with her books, her computer and her cats, Princess Winifred and Princess Grace. In her spare time she enjoys sewing, movies, talking on the phone with her sister, and directing plays and musicals. She has written nearly ninety books for Harlequin.

Books by Kate Hoffmann

Harlequin Blaze

Seducing the Marine

The Mighty Quinns

The Mighty Quinns: Jack
The Mighty Quinns: Rourke
The Mighty Quinns: Dex
The Mighty Quinns: Malcolm
The Mighty Quinns: Rogan
The Mighty Quinns: Ryan
The Mighty Quinns: Eli
The Mighty Quinns: Devin
The Mighty Quinns: Mac

To get the inside scoop on Harlequin Blaze and its talented writers, be sure to check out BlazeAuthors.com.

All backlist available in ebook format.

Visit the Author Profile page at Harlequin.com for more titles.

1

"SAMUEL JEFFERSON BLACKSTONE! Where are you?"

Sam winced at the sound of his younger sister's voice as it echoed through the ground floor of the Blackstone Inn. He gave the pipe wrench one last twist, then wriggled out of the cupboard.

"I'm in here," he called. "In the kitchen."

By the time Sarah reached the kitchen, he was washing his hands in the newly repaired sink. At least he'd thought it was fixed until he heard the unmistakable drip of a leaky drainpipe. Sam cursed softly.

This was one of those moments when he was painfully reminded that the Blackstone Inn didn't come close to turning a profit from year to year. If it did, he could call a real plumber to take care of these nagging maintenance problems. But Sam couldn't recall a time in his life when the inn had provided more than a meager living to the person who owned it—and right now that guy was him.

"Is it fixed?" Sarah asked.

"Not yet," he muttered.

"Did you use the goop and the strips?"

He shook his head. "Just the goop."

Sarah rolled her eyes and shook her head. "I told you to use the strips, too. That's how James fixed it the last time."

Sam glanced over at his sister. "Maybe you could call James and invite him over to dinner? Take him to a movie and then just casually mention our leaky pipes?"

"Do you really want my entire dating life taken up by romancing the various craftsmen around town?" Sarah asked, grabbing an apple from the wood bowl on the counter. "I've dated electricians, roofers, carpenters, masons… I draw the line at plumbers."

"James seems like a nice guy," Sam commented. "And it would be very helpful if you married someone handy. That would solve all our problems."

"I'm not going to date James." Sarah pushed away from the counter. "Besides, you and I both know exactly what would solve our problems. And since you refuse to find a ridiculously wealthy wife, it's going to be at least another twenty-five years of this."

A wife with deep pockets would certainly help, Sam mused. But why would a woman with money saddle herself with an old inn and a husband who was tied to it like a ship to an anchor? This was his burden. Why would he wish it on any woman, especially a woman he loved?

"You don't have to stick around," Sam said. "The inn isn't your problem."

She shrugged. "I don't have anywhere better to be

right now. And if I leave, who is going to cook the meals for our demanding guests?" Sarah started out of the kitchen, then stopped. "Oh, I thought you should know. I saw moving vans parked in front of Abigail Farnsworth's house. It looks like they're finally clearing her stuff out. You might want to go get the George Washington bed before they cart it away."

"Jerry Harrington told me they'd call me when I could pick it up," Sam said.

"I'm not sure I'd trust him with something so important."

"He's our cousin."

"Oh, good Lord," Sarah said. "Half the people in this town are related to us in some distant way. Abby Farnsworth is our third cousin twice removed."

"Fourth," he corrected. Sam grabbed his keys out of his pocket and hurried to the door. "Stick the bucket back under the sink to catch that leak. I'll get on it later." He sighed as he remembered all the other repairs the old building needed urgently.

The Blackstone Inn was the third oldest inn in the state of New York and the only one of the three in continuous operation since the time of the Revolutionary War. It sat on a beautiful bluff above the Hudson River on the outskirts of the town of Millhaven.

It had been built by Sam's seventh great-grandfather, added to by his sixth and fifth great-grandfathers, and been passed down for nine generations to the eldest son of the eldest son in the family.

During the Revolutionary War, the inn was an important military landmark on the road between New

York City and Albany, and north to Quebec City. After
the war, it was a waypoint for settlers moving into the
northern reaches of the state. And then, in 1797, when
Albany was named the capital of the state, it became a
favorite spot for traveling politicians and businessmen.

Sam steered the truck into the quaint environs of
the town. He had grown up in Millhaven and from a
young age he'd known that his future was predeter-
mined. He was the eldest son of an eldest son and, as
such, the Blackstone Inn was his birthright.

There were moments when he felt the burden of his
family's history, much like a royal might chafe against
a life of duty. For a long time he'd tried to find a way
out, but his father and grandfather had both put in their
years at the helm. It was his turn now. And there was
no out.

If Sam walked away, his father, Joseph, would be
forced out of retirement to run the inn, and when he
died, a family committee would choose an heir—most
likely Sarah. His sister had so much talent, Sam didn't
want her to be tied to an old inn in a small town. So
Sam accepted his legacy with gritted teeth and a tight
smile. He'd do his duty for as long as he could.

When he pulled the pickup to a stop in front of Abigail's house, he paused before getting out. The George
Washington bed had become a symbol of the ups and
downs of the Blackstone Inn. Over the years it had
been sold and reacquired three times, often to rela-
tives. Sam's grandfather had been the last to sell it.
Faced with a financial crisis, he'd finally accepted Abigail Farnsworth's offer, but only because Abigail had

promised to return the bed completely free of charge once she'd gotten her money's worth out of it. Which was now, Sam hoped.

He hopped out of the truck and wove his way through the crowd of onlookers bundled against the February chill. As the tangle of moving men removed each beautiful antique, the crowd had a chance to see the life's work of one the state's most respected collectors. After a recent hip injury, Abigail Farnsworth had decided to join her sister, Emily, and retire to the warmer climate of Phoenix, Arizona. And today many of her precious antiques were headed for the auction block.

Sam spotted one of the workmen with the headboard from his bed and he hurried over, only to be brushed aside by a woman dressed entirely in black.

"You can put that in the back of the trailer," she said. "Make sure to wrap it with the moving quilts. Do you have the side rails?"

"Hey!" Sam shouted. "Hold up there." The workman looked up at him as Sam approached. "Where are you going with that bed?"

The guy shrugged. "I'm just following orders," he said.

"That's my bed," Sam said.

The woman turned to face him and the moment their eyes met Sam felt his breath slowly leave his body. She was one of those women you wanted to meet only on your best day, when you'd bothered to shave that morning and put on something other than faded jeans and a T-shirt. And when you had something terribly interesting to say if the conversation lagged—as it just had.

She shifted her sunglasses down on the bridge of her nose and studied him with eyes the color of expensive cognac. Everything about her seemed to ooze elegance, from her dark hair pulled into a loose knot at her nape to her perfect profile, clear testament to generations of careful breeding. A shiver coursed through his body and Sam shifted uneasily.

She's way out of your league, buddy.

"There must be some mistake," she murmured, her eyebrow arched.

Sam reached up and ran his fingers through his tousled hair, then forced a smile. "That's my bed," he repeated.

"This bed?" she asked. "No, no. This is my bed."

Sam reached into his pocket and pulled out the letter that Abigail had written, gifting him what they'd affectionately called "The GW."

"I have a letter here from the current owner, Abigail Farnsworth."

She frowned, then pulled out a paper of her own. "I also have a letter from Miss Farnsworth. But mine states that she wishes the bed to go to the Mapother Museum of Decorative Arts in Boston. I'm here to collect it and take it back to Boston."

"Over my dead body," Sam said.

She glanced at the workman. "Put it in the trailer," she ordered.

"If you know what's good for you, you'll leave it right there," Sam warned the man. He glanced around and caught sight of the town lawyer, Jerry Wright, standing on the front porch. "Stay here," he said to the mover. "I'm going to get someone to sort this all out."

As he walked away, Sam glanced over his shoulder at the woman in black. She'd removed her sunglasses and their eyes met again, and she quickly looked away. Sam smiled to himself. It was the first sign of weakness that she'd shown. The attraction wasn't just one-sided. What was going through her pretty head? he wondered.

"Jerry! Get over here."

"Sam, I was just about to call you."

Sam cursed. "Sure you were. Come here and fix this. Some woman from Boston is trying to take my bed. The bed Abigail promised to return to the Blackstone."

Jerry hurried down the porch steps and walked across the lawn to Sam's side. "It seems that Miss Abigail made a lot of promises she didn't tell me about, Sam. Half the stuff in that house is promised to more than one party and now I'm left to untangle this can of worms."

"I don't care about any of that. All I want is the bed."

The other man sighed. "All right, come on."

When they reached the bed, the footboard was already inside the woman's trailer and the mover was just about to load the side rails. "Take that out of there," Jerry ordered. "That bed isn't going anywhere. At least not today."

"I'm afraid you're wrong," the woman said, rounding the back of what could only be her black Lexus SUV. She held out her hand to Jerry. "I'm Amelia Sheffield, Mapother Museum of Decorative Arts. I have this letter from Miss Farnsworth gifting the bed to our museum."

"It's not hers to give away," Sam said. "That bed has been in my family for generations and it's coming back where it belongs."

She studied him for a long moment, like a fighter evaluating her opponent. "And you are?"

"Sam Blackstone."

"Oh, yes. I've read the bed's provenance. You sold the antique to Abigail. I'm afraid I didn't see that you'd purchased it back. There would have been paperwork, no?"

Sam let his gaze drift over her beautiful features. "My grandfather, also named Samuel Blackstone, sold the bed. Let's just call Abigail and find out what she thinks."

"I doubt that would solve anything," Jerry said. "She seems to be legally obligated to both of you."

"Who had the first claim?" Sam asked. He held out his letter and compared it to Amelia Sheffield's. "I do."

"But wouldn't this be like a will?" Amelia asked. "In that case, the last draft supersedes all others and my letter would be the valid document."

"I'm not going to be the one to decide this," Jerry said. "For now we'll take the bed to a secure storage facility, along with the other disputed pieces of furniture, and figure this out later."

"That's unacceptable," Amelia said. "We're counting on this piece for an exhibit that opens next week. The day after President's Day."

"That's not going to happen," Sam said.

"Will you just…go away? I need this bed and it's mine by right."

"Not a chance. You think I'm just going to give up because you've got a nice smile and a sexy voice?"

She gasped. "What did you say?"

"Oh, don't pretend to be shocked. I saw you checking me out earlier. There's nothing wrong with admitting that you're attracted to me."

"Attracted to *you*? Has anyone ever told you that you're delusional?"

Sam chuckled. He usually wasn't this bold with a woman but he needed to keep Amelia Sheffield off balance. She was a threat, to his business and to centuries-old tradition. And he was enjoying flirting with her.

It didn't take her long to return the volley and they continued to throw verbal hand grenades until a small crowd had gathered around them. Finally Minerva Threadwell stepped forward. Sam groaned as she pulled out her notepad. Minerva was editor of the local newspaper and her husband, Wilbur, ran the local radio station. They were the king and queen of Millhaven gossip.

"I understand there's a dispute over the ownership of the George Washington bed," Minerva said. "Would either of you care to comment?"

"No," Sam said.

At the same time Amelia said, "Yes, I would. My name is Amelia Sheffield and I am from the Mapother Museum of Decorative Arts. Our attorneys have looked over the gift letter quite carefully and they assure me that everything is completely in order. The bed will be going to our museum in Boston."

Minerva turned to Sam, an inquisitive look on her face.

"No comment," he muttered.

"We'll hold on to it for now until this can be resolved," Jerry said.

Sam waited until the movers had shifted the bed from the Mapother trailer into one of the moving vans, then gave them very specific instructions to treat it carefully. As he climbed into his truck, he took a last look back and saw her leaning against the Lexus, her arms crossed over her chest.

Sam took a ragged breath. He felt exactly as he had the day he'd been out hiking along the cliffs overlooking the Hudson and the rock beneath his feet had sheared off. In a split second his life had flashed before his eyes and he'd been sure that he was about to tumble into the abyss. At the last moment he'd stumbled back and away from the edge.

It was the same sensation now, as if he'd managed to escape from some terrible danger.

Amelia Sheffield was too beautiful, too sophisticated, and exactly the kind of woman he found intriguing.

"Walk away, Sam," he murmured. "Just walk away."

"I'M GOING TO have to stay here until I've removed the roadblock," Amelia said, leaning against the driver's-side door of the SUV. "The minute I leave town, this guy is going to take that bed, I know it. And they say, possession is nine-tenths of the law."

"This is not an important piece," her boss, Vivian Brown, said. "Can you afford to be out of the office?"

"I can work from the road for a few days," Amelia told her. "You won't need me on-site until setup. I have everything here on my computer, so give me a chance. I don't want to let this go."

Vivian sighed. "I hired you because of your tenacity. I suppose that's why I ought to let you see this through. You're like a bulldog. You never give up."

"Arf?" Amelia replied.

Vivian chuckled. "Stay as long as you need to. It seems I want that bed as much as you do now."

"Thank you," Amelia said. "I'll get it. I promise."

She disconnected the call and breathed a sigh of relief.

Her boss was right. The bed wasn't an important piece. It was not as if it had been designed especially for George Washington or that it had resided at Mount Vernon. It was just an old bed that Washington had slept in on occasion.

She frowned, remembering Sam Blackstone's accusation that she was attracted to him. Was she simply looking for a reason to extend her stay? She could go back to Boston and let the lawyers deal with it.

No, that man had picked a fight and Amelia wouldn't back down. There was too much riding on this job. Her future, her security; the chance to make her own choices in life.

She hadn't always possessed such an independent streak. As the only child of a notable Boston Brahmin family, she'd been carefully groomed to be sweet and compliant, the kind of girl who would grow up to marry well and transfer the family fortune to an equally wealthy family who would preserve it for future generations.

She'd host luncheons and cocktail parties, she'd bear clever and handsome children, she'd serve on the boards of at least three charitable foundations and she'd see her children married well, too. It had taken her nearly twenty-two years to realize that she wasn't really a person at all, but a prize.

She'd had the traditional education for a girl of her station: a private, all-girls day school, four years at Miss Porter's, then an art history degree from Sarah Lawrence. Though it had been a good education, it had also been a case study in maintaining the chastity of a naïve young girl. The first time she'd even touched a boy she'd been thirteen and taking dance lessons for her tea dance at the club.

She'd led such a silly life as a teenager, paraded around in a white gown and gloves, her hair sprayed until it barely moved, a smile pasted on her face to indicate she was having fun. Inside she'd felt as though she was on display for all the mothers to judge: Amelia Gardner Sheffield, heiress in search of a husband. Only blue bloods need apply.

And she'd followed her parents' plan almost all the way to the altar before she'd realized she was capable of making her own decisions.

Since she'd walked out on her engagement, she'd been determined to make a success of herself without her family's intervention. She'd managed to get the job at the museum without any promises besides hard work and dedication. It was only after she'd been hired that she'd mentioned her family connections.

And until this crazy bed situation had come along, she'd delivered on every project she'd taken on. Now that she'd set her sights on the George Washington bed, she wouldn't leave town until it was tucked safely in the museum's trailer.

But there were some roadblocks along the way. For one thing, she didn't know anything about her opponent. She'd be much more effective against him if she learned something of his motivations. Millhaven was a small town. Certainly someone in town would be willing to talk about Sam Blackstone.

He wanted that bed as much as she did, maybe even more. Unfortunately he wasn't aware of just how stubborn and single-minded Amelia Gardner Sheffield could be.

Amelia opened the door of the Lexus and got in behind the wheel. She'd made the three-hour drive to Millhaven from Boston that morning and had had the presence of mind to pack an overnight bag in case the weather or the acquisition suddenly went bad.

But a bag was only part of the equation; she'd need to find someplace close to spend the night. Millhaven was a quaint little village set in the beauty of the Hudson Valley. There had to be a motel somewhere in town.

As she drove away from the Farnsworth house, she saw a signpost and slowed to read it. It listed three restaurants and one inn.

"The Blackstone Inn." She remembered the bed's provenance mentioning the Blackstone Inn, but it had never occurred to her that the inn would still be in existence. Could Sam Blackstone be connected to the Blackstone Inn? She smiled to herself. "I guess we'll find out soon enough."

The road followed the river and she found the inn about a half mile from the edge of town, set high on a bluff overlooking the Hudson. As Amelia drove up to the front door, she marveled at the view. It was an idyllic spot and more than romantic.

"'Established 1769,'" she read on the sign. Her gaze dropped to a scroll along the bottom of the sign with the words *George Washington slept here*.

"No wonder he wants the bed back," she murmured.

The central structure was made of a type of red brick common throughout the area. The inn was three stories high, the façade featuring three Federal columns flanking each side of the front door and supporting a third-story gallery. It looked as though the two wings on either side of the central structure had been added at a later date, as the bricks were a slightly different color. Black shutters adorned the first-story windows, while window boxes filled with winter greenery marked each second-story window.

Amelia loved it on sight. She quickly got out of the SUV, anxious to see if the interior was as meticulously preserved as the exterior. She admired people who worked so hard to protect historical buildings. Their work was as important as the work she and the rest of the staff did at the Mapother.

Amelia stepped through the front door into a wide Colonial keeping room. On one side a hearth dominated the entire wall, with period chairs and sofas arranged neatly in front of the fire. On the other side a wood-paneled bar ran the depth of the room, the bottles and glassware sparkling beneath the flickering light of four kerosene lamps.

She walked to the front desk and rang the bell that sat on the scarred wooden counter. A few seconds later a young woman emerged from behind a door. There was something very familiar about her pale blue eyes and dark hair. She smiled and Amelia had the uneasy feeling that they'd met before.

"Good afternoon," the other woman said with a warm smile. "May I help—"

"You will not believe what is going on down at Abigail's place." A familiar voice filled the room and Amelia's spine stiffened. "That crazy old lady promised the bed to someone else. Some uptight, snooty museum lady from Boston. Amelia Sheffield. La-di-da. Man, what a piece of work."

Amelia slowly turned and faced him. "Hello again."

The woman behind the desk cleared her throat. "This is my brother, Sam Blackstone." She laughed softly. "And I'd bet you're Amelia Sheffield."

Amelia held out her hand to Sam. "Hello. Piece. Piece of Work. A pleasure to meet you, Mr. Blackstone."

He at least had the grace to show some embarrassment. His face flushed beneath his deep tan and scruffy beard. He really wasn't the type she was usually attracted to but there was something about him that piqued her curiosity.

Maybe it was the fact that he seemed so intent on

obtaining a historical piece of furniture that he'd be rude to a complete stranger to get it. It was exactly the way she felt about important furniture: obsessed.

"So, you own this place?" she asked.

"My sister and I do," he said, nodding to the woman standing at the desk. "My sister, Sarah Blackstone."

Amelia turned and offered Sarah her hand. "Amelia Sheffield. Mapother Museum of Decorative Arts. Boston."

Sarah shook her hand, then stepped out from behind the counter. "I'm just going to leave your check-in to Sam. He'll get you a room. Dinner is at six. There's a menu in your room. Just call down with your choices before five."

"Sarah is a great cook," Sam said.

Amelia regarded Sam suspiciously. "You don't get anywhere near the food, do you?"

"Do you think I'm going to spit in it?" he asked.

"No, of course not. I was more worried about poison."

Sarah laughed again as she headed toward the kitchen. Sam waited until the door swung shut behind her, then turned and stepped behind the front desk. "You'd like to spend the night?"

"That's why I'm here," she said. "Do you have a problem with me taking a room?"

"Not at all," he said. "Everyone is welcome here."

"Are you busy?"

"We have just six guests tonight, so we can give you our full attention."

"Good," she said. Amelia pulled her wallet from her purse and grabbed her business credit card, placing it on the counter between them. "I'd like to see the inn and choose a room for myself. Would you give me a tour?"

He glanced up, as if surprised by her request. "Sure. Why don't we leave your bag here? The rooms in the oldest part of the inn are smaller, but many of them contain original Federal furnishings."

"That sounds perfect," Amelia said.

He followed her up the stairs and she couldn't help but wonder what he was looking at as they climbed to the second story. All the doors were open and she strolled down the narrow hall, peeking inside each room.

The drapery and upholstery fabrics were a bit timeworn and faded, but very well chosen. Beautiful Federal-era beds dominated each room, the canopies reaching the high ceilings. Comfortable wing chairs sat in front of the small fireplaces and each room contained a small writing desk and a pair of bedside tables with oil lamps.

"We have electric lamps," he said, "but a lot of our guests enjoy the true Colonial experience. I can switch the lamps out if you like."

"No, I love antique lamps." When they reached the corner room at the end of the hall, Amelia paused before entering the room. "This is nice."

"There are shared bathrooms in this part of the inn," he said. "The new rooms are en suite."

"The shared bath is fine," Amelia said. "I'm only here for a night." She walked into the room and nodded. "Yes, I'll stay here."

"Funny," Sam said. "This is the George Washington

bedroom. The bed that you want to steal used to be in this room. George Washington slept right here."

Sam smiled—the first true smile he'd given her—and it was dazzling. Her pulse began to beat faster and she felt a bit light-headed.

"I'll just go get your bag," he said and left the room.

Once the door shut behind him Amelia let out a tightly held breath. She sank down onto the edge of the bed and folded her hands on her lap. Until this moment she hadn't realized the energy it took to maintain a calm and composed nature when he was standing next to her.

There was a current of anticipation that pulsed inside her, like an electrical current that threatened to spark and ignite if he touched her…or kissed her. Amelia groaned softly and pressed her fingertips to her lips.

Maybe that's why she'd decided to stay. To see if he'd kiss her. As he'd led her through the rooms, she'd caught his gaze lingering on her mouth, as if he were thinking about it. Or was that all just in her imagination? Emotions ran so high between them it was hard to tell what it all meant.

And if they did succumb to curiosity or desire or passion, what then? It would only complicate an already tangled relationship. Maybe it was a mistake to stay, Amelia mused. She was only tempting fate. But, oh, what a fate…

"What are you thinking?" Amelia flopped back onto the bed and stared up at the coffered ceiling. "Stop all these silly fantasies."

A knock sounded on her room door and she jumped

to her feet, smoothing her hair as she walked to the door. Sam was waiting on the other side with her bag. He held it out to her. "Dinner is at six. The menu is on that table over there. Just call down to the kitchen and let Sarah know what you'd like."

"Thank you," she said. But he didn't leave. Should she give him a tip? Maybe that's what he was waiting for. Amelia grabbed her purse and took a step toward him. Sam took a step back.

"Well, I'll see you at dinner, then," Sam said and closed the door.

Amelia stepped up to it, pressing her forehead against the cool, painted wood.

"Is she out there?" Sam asked. He peered through the small window of the kitchen door but he couldn't see the entire dining room from his viewpoint. "What did she order?"

"Fillet of beef, potatoes Anna and the house salad with Gorgonzola. She's also put away two glasses of our best red wine and six slices of bread with butter. Would you like me to go out and get her pulse and temperature for you?"

"She's not a vegetarian, that's good."

"Good for what?" Sarah asked.

Sam shook his head and turned away from the door. "I don't know. What difference does it make?"

Sarah slid a pie pan across the kitchen island. "Why don't you take her some dessert? There's ice cream in the freezer and whipped cream in the fridge. If she wants coffee, you know how to make it. And you can

take care of the dishes tonight. I've got Pilates class."
Sarah walked out, leaving him alone in the kitchen.

He'd been searching for an opportunity to speak to
Amelia again since her arrival at the inn. He'd been
tempted to check on her during the afternoon but hadn't
wanted to appear as if he were hovering.

Millhaven was a small town and it was almost impossible for him to have a social life. Sam knew almost
everyone in the village who was single and around his
own age. Since he'd come back to the inn four years
ago he'd gone from an unrepentant skirt-chaser as a
college undergrad to Mr. Responsible. He wasn't even
sure if he remembered how to flirt.

And he'd need to be at the top of his game for Amelia Sheffield. He sensed that it would take a lot more
than prompt service and homemade desserts to break
through her icy façade. She probably expected to be en-
tertained with witty chitchat or intrigued by important
conversation about art or current events. But Sam had
never been comfortable at cocktail parties. His charm
was more homegrown, rising out of the humor of the
moment. Then again, they weren't at a cocktail party.
They were in *his* inn. His territory.

He placed the pie, plates and forks, and the can of
whipped cream on a tray, then carried it out into the
dining room. When Amelia saw him, her gaze followed
his path as he wove through the dining room tables to
where she sat.

Though she was still dressed in black, she'd let her
hair down and it fell in soft waves around her face, the
color a deep mahogany that set off the gold in her eyes.

She didn't wear a lot of makeup and her simple, clean beauty was much more attractive to him than the paint and perfume that some women chose to use.

"I know you're happy to see me," he said, smiling at her.

"I am?"

"I brought pie. My sister's apple pie. Made from the Cortland apples we grow right here on our property. They're the best."

"I love Cortland apples," she said. "They're so hard to find these days. And I'll admit I'm always happy when pie enters the room."

"Mind if I join you?"

She hesitated at first, then quickly shook her head. "No, sit," she said, indicating the chair across from her.

But Sam grabbed the chair beside her and sat, placing the tray in front of him. "Did you enjoy the dinner?"

"Are we really going to talk about food? I thought you'd prefer to get right down to negotiating," she said.

He scooped up a generous slice of the pie and plopped it on a plate, which he handed to her. "There's nothing to negotiate. I know that Abigail will clear this up and the bed will come home with me."

"I have every faith in our lawyers," she countered.

If the fight came down to lawyers, Sam would lose. He didn't have the money to hire Jerry to represent him in a lengthy court case. The inn operated on a shoestring that didn't include hundred-dollar-an-hour lawyers. "Why is it so important you get this bed?"

"George Washington slept in it," she replied.

"The bed has been in my family since it was first made. Doesn't that mean something to you?"

"Sure it does," she said. "But you want to close the bed up in a little room here at the inn. I want to show it to the public."

"What exactly do you do for this museum of yours, besides pillaging the countryside and stealing people's furniture?"

"I acquire items for our exhibits," she said.

Sam chuckled. "Oh, well, that sounds so much better. You *acquire*."

"How we lived is just as important as what we lived. I help to preserve that," Amelia said. She paused, as if to gather her thoughts, then continued in a less aggressive tone. "You of all people should understand. You live in a monument to history. Look at this place. It's perfect."

Sam glanced around. He couldn't remember the last time he'd attached the word *perfect* to the Blackstone Inn.

She continued. "My last exhibition was called 'Cabin in the Woods.' I set up three interiors of rustic Colonial-era frontier homes, complete with everything it would take to live in the wilderness. But it was interactive, so children could touch and experience everything. It fired their imagination, and that's really all that's left to us of history. Museums, a few historic inns and homes like yours, and our imaginations."

He heard the passion in her words and admired her dedication. She even made him feel some pride in his own work at the inn, and it had been a long time since he'd held any sort of affection toward the Blackstone. "And this place is called the Mapother Museum?"

"Of Decorative Arts. It focuses on interior décor—furniture, china, linens, rugs and ceramics. The kind of place that draws busloads of retired ladies and interior designers," she added.

"I still don't understand why you have to 'acquire' my bed," he said. "Any piece from the period should do."

"Have we determined that it is *your* bed?"

"The bed has belonged to my family since the inn opened. Abigail bought it when we were short of funds, but she promised to return it to its rightful place."

"We're opening a new children's exhibit about George Washington for President's Day. The bed will be the perfect centerpiece for the gallery. Kids could lie on it and take photos, and we'll get lots of publicity. Which is always good for the museum."

"So my bed is going to be a…a historical bouncy house? Why not throw any old bed into the exhibit? No one is going to know any better."

"I have a reputation for authenticity to protect," she said. "And I can't be sentimental."

"I think a better word might be *sympathetic* or *kind*."

"You can't make me feel guilty," she said.

"What can I make you feel?" he asked. The moment the words slipped out of his mouth, Sam realized his mistake. What the hell was he thinking? A cultured woman like Amelia would never respond to such a suggestive comment.

"I—I'm not sure I understand what you mean," she murmured.

"I should get back to work," he said quickly. "Is there anything else I can get you, Ms. Sheffield?"

"No," she murmured. "I'm quite content, Mr. Blackstone."

He got up and walked to the kitchen, refusing to look back. *So much for charm*, Sam mused. He'd been right the first time: it was going to take a lot more than awkward small talk and apple pie to seduce Amelia Sheffield. He had one more day to figure this all out. One day to take this attraction beyond the theoretical to something real. Or else she'd be on her way back to Boston—with his bed.

2

AMELIA STARED UP at the ceiling of her room at the Blackstone Inn. Somewhere deep inside the darkened inn, a grandfather clock chimed. She counted three chimes, then threw her arm over her eyes. But nothing she did helped her find the peace of sleep.

She sat up, tossed aside the down-filled pillow and swung her legs off the bed. She needed something to eat. Just a little something to get her through until breakfast. Her mind was racing with thoughts of work and Sam Blackstone; a confusing jumble that didn't make any sense no matter how hard she tried to put it all in order.

She grabbed her sweater and pulled it on over her T-shirt and yoga pants, then searched her bag for something to put on her feet. She found a pair of socks and slipped them on. Dragging a deep breath, she snuck out into the dimly lit hall and headed for the stairs.

The stairs creaked with each step she took and Amelia winced, wondering just how far away the family slept. She assumed they had quarters somewhere in one of the newer wings. By the time she reached the kitchen, her heart was pounding and she was breathless.

"Apple pie," she murmured. She and Sam had taken the first two pieces of the freshly baked pie. All the other guests had eaten and left the dining room by the time Amelia had finished. So the rest of the pie had to be around somewhere. Amelia searched the refrigerator first but all she found was the can of whipped cream. A search of the freezer resulted in a carton of vanilla ice cream. But there was no pie.

Amelia glanced around the kitchen and noticed an old pie safe. Tall and narrow, the ancient cabinet sat in a spot near the stone hearth. She walked over to it and ran her hand across the pierced tin panels on the door. Of course the pie would be in the pie safe.

To her surprise there was also a raspberry pie tucked in beneath the apple. She pulled them both out, set them on the island and grabbed a dinner plate and fork from the drying rack beside the sink.

The pie tasted as good as it had earlier that evening, and Amelia's thoughts drifted back to the man who'd shared her table in the dining room.

She'd only ever had one boyfriend in her life and to say that Sam Blackstone was his exact opposite was stating the absolute truth.

Her thoughts shifted to Edward. She wasn't really sure what to call him anymore. He'd been her boyfriend, then her fiancé and then her ex-fiancé and then her friend. He'd said he'd wait for her, but as time passed, their relationship had grown more and more distant.

Amelia took another bite of the pie and sighed softly. Edward Ardmore Reed the Third. Heir to an old and very successful Boston banking dynasty. He'd been the only man she'd ever loved. At least she'd thought she'd loved him. But he'd been her parents' choice from a very early age. She hadn't even dated anyone else. And when she'd broken from her parents' control, she'd ended her engagement, as well.

In her anger and frustration, she'd thrown him in with her parents, certain that he'd try to control her life the moment her parents signed her over to him. He'd always been good to her, but Amelia wanted more.

They'd stayed in touch over the past year and Amelia knew that he hadn't given up hope she'd come to her senses. But though there was affection between them, there had never been any heat or passion.

"Can't sleep?"

The sound of his voice startled her and she spun around to find Sam watching her from the shadows. Her heart skipped a beat, then began pounding in earnest. "I—I didn't see you there." Amelia looked around, embarrassed to be caught raiding the kitchen. "I'm sorry. I'm a late-night snacker. I can't sleep if I'm hungry."

"It's all right," he said, stepping forward. "If you need anything, you just have to call."

He was dressed only in a pair of basketball shorts that were slung low on his hips. His chest was bare, as were his feet. A tiny shiver skittered through her and her fingers twitched, eager to trace the muscles of his chest. "Would you like some?" Amelia asked.

"Sure."

He pulled out a stool and sat at the island. "It's been kind of a crazy day," he murmured as he watched Amelia cut into the pie.

"Pretty crazy," she repeated. "Not the typical day in the life of an innkeeper."

"It's an exciting life," he muttered, a sarcastic edge in his voice. "Just what a guy like me always dreamed about."

"You didn't want to be an innkeeper?"

Sam took a bite of the pie. "Maybe at some point in my life. But not at twenty-five. To be tied down to one place for the rest of my life is kind of a daunting prospect."

"Can't you sell the inn?"

He shook his head. "This is a family business. It's passed down from generation to generation, from the first son to the first son. And I got lucky. If I'd been the second son of the second son, I could have been an architect. Building great buildings instead of fixing leaky pipes."

"You have Sarah to help you."

"She stays out of guilt."

"Why?"

"The tradition is that the inn is passed along in a person's later years, almost like a job for retirement. I got it about thirty years early because my father and stepmother wanted out."

"What about your mother?"

"They divorced when I was ten," he said. "My mother never wanted the whole inn-keeping life. It's a twenty-four-hour-a-day job. The demands never go away." He sighed deeply, then rubbed his eyes. "I'm sorry. I shouldn't complain. Hell, I have a job and it's not like I'm digging ditches for a living." Sam pushed back from the counter. "I'm just going to leave you to your pie."

"Don't," she said, reaching out to grab his hand. "I like the company."

"The grumpy company?"

"You're not grumpy." She smiled. "Well, maybe a little bit. But that's what the pie is for. Pie always brightens one's spirits. Look at that cabinet over there. It's quite a wonderful piece. A Colonial-era pie safe."

"You've been examining our antiques?"

"I can't help myself," Amelia said. "It's what I do. And I can tell you that I wish I had that pie safe in our collection. It's gorgeous."

"It was a wedding present from my seventh great-grandfather to his new wife. There's an inscription carved in the back."

"That's amazing," she said. "Do you have more? I'd love to go through the inn and see everything you have. Especially in the attic."

"I'll take you on a private tour," he said.

"I'd like that," she said. Amelia looked and realized they'd made a big dent in the pie. "I think I'd come back here just for the pie."

"It's an authentic Colonial recipe," he said. "Right down to the lard. My sister believes that if you're going to stay in an eighteenth-century inn, you need to be prepared to eat like they did then."

"I admire that you've dedicated yourselves to authenticity. It's honest and pure."

They stared at each other for a long moment. Amelia finally broke her gaze away from his and stood, placing her hands flat on the counter. "I should go to bed."

"When are you going back to Boston?" he asked.

"When my bed is packed in the trailer," she teased. "Do you want to get rid of me? That's how you can do it. Pack it up and I'll be out of here."

"No, I don't want to get rid of you," he said with a grin. "I'm starting to like having you around. You make things interesting." Sam reached out and took her hand. "Come on, I'll walk you up to your room."

They strolled through the dining room and the keeping room, the old plank floors creaking beneath their feet. When they reached the second floor, she had to walk ahead of him through the narrow hallway. They stood in front of her door for a long moment and Amelia noticed how dark it was in the hallway—how private, intimate.

He placed his hands on the wall on either side of her head. "It's been an interesting day," he murmured, his gaze scanning her features in the dim light.

"Yes, it has," Amelia said.

"Kind of a change of pace for me."

"Really?"

Sam nodded. "You're the most exciting thing that's happened to me in a long time." His gaze moved to her lips. "I'm going to kiss you now," he whispered, leaning close. His lips brushed against hers. It was so sweet, so simple, that she wanted it to go on forever. But Sam seemed determined to leave her needing more. He stepped back and smiled. "Good night, Amelia. Sleep tight."

"Sam?" she called out.

He looked over his shoulder. "Yeah?"

"Do you kiss all your guests good-night?"

He chuckled softly. "No. You're the first."

He continued down the hall. Amelia's knees started to buckle and she leaned against the door for balance. This was what Sam Blackstone did to her. He kept her completely off balance, until she really wasn't sure what was up and what was down. And she was starting to enjoy the feeling.

JERRY HAD CALLED early that morning with the news that he'd spoken to Abigail Farnsworth and she'd made a decision. He'd asked Sam to meet him at the warehouse. When Sam had asked about Amelia, Jerry had told him that he'd contact her, as well, but Sam decided to take the initiative.

He climbed the stairs to the second floor, a mug of hot coffee in his hand, and walked down the hall to her room. He paused, his mind rewinding to the kiss they'd shared in the predawn hours.

Sam had never been an impulsive guy, especially when it came to women. But Amelia was unlike any other woman he'd met. From the moment he'd set eyes on her, he'd felt as though a clock had begun ticking, measuring out the minutes and hours they had together.

He had no time to contemplate every move he made. When he'd felt the urge to kiss her, he'd had to act. To his surprise, she'd seemed pleased that he'd kissed her. But he wondered if that feeling would survive the light of day. Well, he was sure he could find a pleasurable way to convince her.

Sam rapped on the door and waited. A few seconds later it swung open and Amelia greeted him with a soft, "Hi." She brushed the dark strands of her hair out of her eyes and smiled.

"Morning," Sam said, holding out the coffee. "I wasn't sure how you took it. Black. I hope that's all right."

"Perfect," she said.

"There's something I need to talk to you about. Do you have a few minutes?"

"What time is it?" Amelia asked.

"A little past eight." Sam paused. "I just got a call from Jerry. He wanted me to meet him at the warehouse. He has news from Abigail."

"How did he know I was here?"

"He didn't," Sam said. "And he didn't specifically ask that you be there. But I think you should, since whatever he has to say will affect you as well as me. So, I'm going to leave in about ten minutes. If you want to hear what he has to say, meet me down in the lobby."

"I do want to know," Amelia replied. "Thank you."

He shrugged. "No problem." Sam stepped back into the hall and, when the door clicked shut, cursed himself softly.

He should have stepped into the room, wrapped his

arm around her waist and kissed her. It was the last chance he'd probably have. Once Amelia found out that the bed was his, she'd immediately head home to Boston.

Sam reached out to knock on the door again but pulled his hand away. He'd make sure there'd be a quiet moment for them sometime before she drove off. Sam turned and walked downstairs. Sarah was just going through the reservations as he passed.

"You're up early," he said.

"We've got that wedding coming in this weekend and I wanted to get a jump on the preparations. I hope you're going to be around today. Our other guests are leaving in the next few hours. I'm going to need your help."

"Sure. I just have to run over and see Jerry about the bed. Then I'm free. When Amelia comes through, tell her to meet me outside in the truck."

"Yes," Sarah murmured. "I will tell the piece of work that you're awaiting her in the truck."

He gave her a dismissive glare and she laughed. Was he that obvious? If Sarah had already picked up on the fact that there was something going on, then the whole town would probably have it figured out within a day. Even more reason to step up his plan to get to know Amelia more intimately.

Sam was still cleaning out the front seat of his truck when Amelia hurried down the porch steps. Yesterday she'd been chic and aloof. Today, dressed in jeans and a fleece pullover, she looked relaxed…and beautiful.

Sam ran around to her side of the truck, opened the

door and then helped her in. As he closed the door, Sam realized that he'd missed another chance to kiss her—and he had very few of those chances left.

Cursing softly, he got into the truck and turned to her. Slipping his fingers around her nape, he gently pulled her toward him. Amelia didn't offer any resistance, and by the time their lips met, hers were slightly parted.

She tasted like sweet toothpaste, cinnamon and coffee. His fingers tangled in her hair as he pulled her more deeply into the kiss. His mind spun and for several long moments he couldn't make himself think rationally. He wanted to stop; he knew he had to. But the kiss continued to spin out of control as they groped for closer contact.

He couldn't explain the attraction. It was part physical, part intellectual. Yes, she was out of his league, but that didn't seem to stop him. Maybe if he could understand what drew him to her, he could find an excuse to stop himself.

Finally Amelia pulled away. She stared out the front windshield, her breath coming in tiny gasps.

"Good morning," Sam murmured.

A tiny smile quirked at the corners of her mouth. "Good morning," she said. She opened the door and jumped to the ground. "I think I'll drive myself."

"You can ride with me," he shouted as she headed toward her Lexus.

"No, I'll take my truck. I'll need the trailer for the bed."

He leaped out of the truck. "You still believe you're going to get the bed?"

"I'm hopeful," she called.

"I think you're going to be disappointed."

Sam watched her start her truck, then hopped back into his own and turned the key in the ignition. He drove silently into town and within a few minutes pulled up in front of an old storefront on Center Street, on the north end of the business district.

Gold letters painted on the huge glass window identified the place as Benny Barnes Antiques and Auction Gallery. Benny, one of the town's more colorful characters, had added his own personal tagline to the window: I Buy Old Stuff.

Benny had agreed to take the bed, along with the other disputed pieces, and hold them until ownership had been determined. Ever the marketing genius, he'd taken the opportunity to get some publicity out of it for himself, setting the Washington bed up in his front window with a lovely hand-painted sign and antique bed linens.

As Sam parked beside her, Amelia hopped out of the truck, not waiting for him to get her door. She stood in front of the wide plate-glass window and Sam joined her.

"Nice to know I can keep an eye on it," Sam muttered.

A worried expression crossed her face and she gnawed on her lower lip. "Right."

He rested his palm on the small of her back as he held the front door open for her and they stepped inside the dimly lit interior. Jerry was waiting for them, stretched out in a tattered wing chair, a mug of coffee in his hands.

"Morning," he said, nodding to the two of them.

"Morning, Jerry," Sam said. "You remember Amelia Sheffield. She stayed at the inn last night, so I let her know about the meeting."

Jerry frowned, glancing back and forth between the two of them. "Will you excuse us, miss?" he said, getting up and grabbing Sam by the arm. He dragged him to a quiet corner of Benny's office. "You're giving aid and refuge to the enemy now?"

"I'm confident we'll prevail," he said. "And she's a paying customer."

"Yeah? Well, you'd best watch yourself. A woman that beautiful is nothing but trouble."

They walked back out to Amelia and found her inside the large display window, examining the details on the bed.

"Well, I've got good news and bad," Jerry began. "Good news is there's no one else making a claim on this piece. Bad news is Miss Abigail has decided to leave the decision up to you two."

"How's that going to work?" Sam asked.

"Hell if I know. But you're going to have to fight this one out yourselves. When you've got it sorted, give me a call and I'll write up the paperwork. Until then, Benny says he'll keep the bed here."

After he walked out, they stood next to each other, silently, both of them weighing their options. Amelia was the first to speak. She removed her phone from her purse. "Where can I buy some bed linens? Sheets and a pillow?"

"Why would you need that?"

"I'm going to stay here, live here in this bed, until you give up your claim. Unless you want to give up right now, which would save us both a lot of time and trouble?"

"I'm not giving up. It's my bed. It's a family heirloom."

"And you thought by seducing me, I might forget that point? Well, I haven't. You can kiss me all you want, Sam Blackstone, and it's not going to shake my determination." She sat on the edge of the bed.

"You want to stay here in this dusty old window?"

"Yes. I hope the store has a bathroom. Why don't you go check on that for me?"

"I'm not going to stay here," Sam said.

"Then you're giving up already?"

"No. But this isn't the way to decide this. We could flip a coin. We could arm wrestle or cut cards. We don't have to live here."

"Well, I am going to live here. I'm going to sleep in my bed until it's all mine."

He cursed beneath his breath. This was crazy. How was it that she was dictating the terms? Hell, they could take the bed back to the inn and live in relative comfort and seclusion.

"Hello! Anyone here?" A moment later Minerva Threadwell came around the corner. She wore a bright purple warm-up suit and had her gray hair pulled into a tidy bun at the top of her head. Rabbit-fur earmuffs covered her ears and she looked as if she'd just happened in on her morning walk. "Oh, here you are. I just got a tip that there was new development on the bed. I can get it into our Thursday edition." She reached into her pocket and pulled out her notepad and pen. "Care to comment?"

Sam groaned. "Is this really what you consider newsworthy, Minerva?"

"It's a small town," she said in a clipped tone. "I take what I can get. So, whose bed is it, yours or hers?"

Amelia pulled a business card out of her pocket. "Amelia Sheffield of the Mapother Museum. And it seems Miss Farnsworth left the decision up to us. So, I'll just be staying here, sleeping in this bed, until Mr. Blackstone agrees to let me take it to Boston for my exhibit."

"Well, this is an interesting development," Minerva said. "Kind of a John Lennon-Yoko Ono thing."

"What?"

"Oh, right," Amelia said. "A sleep-in."

"So you two are going to sleep in the bed together?"

"I'm not sleeping here," Sam protested.

"Then what's to prevent her from taking off with your bed in the middle of the night?" Minerva asked, an inquisitive arch to her eyebrow.

Sam cursed beneath his breath. "I guess I'll be sleeping here with her."

Minerva's smile widened. "Now, that will make the story even more interesting. You'll be sharing the bed?"

"No," Sam and Amelia said at the same time.

Then Sam realized this could be the opportunity

he'd been hoping for. "I mean yes," Sam said. "It's only fair. It is my bed."

"It's my bed and you won't be sleeping in it," Amelia said.

"Which is it?" the reporter asked. "Are you going to sleep together or not?"

"Yes," Amelia said.

The reporter turned to look at Sam. "And…you're all right with that?"

"Sure," Sam said. He sent Amelia a lazy smile. "I don't plan to do a lot of sleeping."

He heard a tiny gasp catch in Amelia's throat and took satisfaction in the realization that he'd managed to rattle her. Miss Cool and Collected had a weak spot. Was she imagining what might happen once the lights went out?

"What's so important about this bed?" Minerva asked.

"George Washington slept in this bed," Amelia said.

"I expect he slept in many beds over the course of his life," Minerva commented.

"It's not very important," Sam countered. "But it's always had a home with the Blackstone family. Ms. Sheffield doesn't seem to understand the value of family traditions."

"Do you have proof that George Washington slept in the bed?"

Amelia nodded. "Of course. Mr. Blackstone's grandfather included paperwork on the provenance with copies of Washington's signature from the inn's guest book. I've done other research, as well."

"Would you care to elaborate?" Minerva said. "I'd also be interested to know the value of the bed."

"On second thought, I could have been wrong," Sam murmured. "Maybe that wasn't the bed in the corner room. I may have confused things."

Minerva looked back and forth between the two of them. "I'd like to send Wilbur over to take a photo. How long do you think it will be before the two of you are in bed together?"

"I'll leave that up to Ms. Sheffield," he said.

"No comment," she murmured, her cheeks flushed with color.

"I have enough for now, anyway," Minerva said. "I know how to contact both of you. If I need anything else, I'll drop by." She sighed. "Wilbur's going to want to get this on the noon news." Minerva tucked her notepad into her pocket and hurried out the front door.

They stood in silence for a long moment before Sam clapped his hands. "All right," he said. "We're on. I say we meet back here at noon with everything we need and then we'll get started."

"All right," Amelia said, tipping her chin up. "The battle for the bed starts at noon. May the best…person win." She held out her hand and he shook it.

She was ready to leave it at that, but he wasn't. Instead he slipped his hand around her waist and pulled her against his body. His lips covered hers in a deep, damp kiss, their tongues creating a delicious connection he didn't want to break. When she pulled away, he looked down into her wide eyes.

"May the best man win," he whispered.

Her expression hardened and she wrapped her hand around his nape and pulled him into another kiss. Her mouth was soft and searching, her tongue tracing the width of his mouth, teasing him in a way that was more provocative than he expected.

The blood in his body warmed and desire flooded his senses. His hands skimmed along her torso and settled on her hips, holding her against him. The friction between them caused an instant reaction in him.

But Amelia wasn't about to let him take control. She stepped away and gave him a coy smile, her lips still damp and glistening. "Don't you mean the best woman?"

AMELIA WATCHED THROUGH the plate-glass window as Sam drove away. When he was finally out of sight, she turned to the bed. By her estimate, it would take about a half hour to disassemble it and get it loaded into the trailer. If he came back at noon, that would give her a half-hour head start to Boston; a half hour before he even realized she was gone.

She didn't regret deceiving him. This was war and she had to use whatever advantage she was given. He'd have done the same thing given the opportunity. She hurried over to the bed and examined it. Getting the canopy off on her own would be difficult, but once that was done, the rest of the bed would come apart quickly.

She crawled up on the mattress and began to untie the stays on the fabric covering. Struggling with a knot, she had a brief flash of conscience, then reminded herself that all was fair in love and war.

Her mind skipped to the kiss they'd shared earlier. His powerful and demanding; hers defiant and daring. Somehow she'd allowed desire to become part of their battle and it wasn't helping her gain the upper hand. Every time he touched her, she felt weak, vulnerable, and yet so amazingly alive that she wanted to cry out. Her body pulsed with a need so powerful it threatened to sweep her away. She'd never experienced anything remotely similar when Edward had kissed her, and he was supposed to be the love of her life.

Her parents had never seemed to share any passion between them and Amelia had always assumed that those emotions were saved for the privacy of their bedroom. But now she realized that it was impossible to hide such intense reactions. She felt her need with every breath she took. She wanted Sam to kiss her, to touch her, to throw her down on the bed and have his way with her.

She cursed softly as she worked at the knot. Amelia Gardner Sheffield was not the kind of woman who wielded her sexuality to get what she wanted. Until she'd met Sam, she hadn't been aware that she had that power at all.

But was it a power she wanted to wield? She could soften him up; make him more amenable to her. And once he'd fallen for her, he'd want to give her the bed. But she'd been manipulated her whole life. She didn't want to do that to someone else.

"You need any help with that?"

The voice startled her and she spun around quickly, losing her balance. A man stood at the foot of the bed, his arms crossed over his chest. He chuckled, then held out his hand. "Benny Barnes. I don't think we've met."

"Oh," Amelia cried, stumbling off the bed. "This is your place. No, we haven't met. Amelia Sheffield. Mapother Museum of Decorative Arts. It's a pleasure to meet you."

"So you're the one fighting with Sammy over this bed," Benny said. "No one mentioned you were such a pretty little thing." He grinned widely. "Can I give you a hand?"

"You could help me take this bed apart and move it into my trailer," she said.

Benny shook his head. "Nah, I'm afraid I can't do that. Unless Sam gives me the word, the bed stays here."

"I see," Amelia said. "You're a friend of his?"

"This is a small town, miss. Everyone is friends with everyone else. Minerva filled me in on the whole situation. I have to say, you've got your work cut out for you. That Sam is used to getting what he wants. We went to high school together. He was a few years younger than me but, yeah, we were good buddies. Wasn't as popular as me or as smart, but we hung out."

Benny puffed out his chest and continued to talk about his high school exploits, nodding and smiling as if she were impressed. Maybe he thought she was. After all, she had invited herself to spend the night in his place of business.

"I'd like to thank you for allowing this to play out in your front window."

"No problem. It'll bring a lot of attention to my

business. As a thank-you, why don't you let me take you out to lunch? Or how about dinner? I can show you around town, introduce you to the right people."

"There is one thing you can do for me," Amelia said with a warm smile. "I could use a sheet or something to hang over the front window. For privacy."

"Well, you can't do that," Benny said. "What would be the point? I gotta promote the hell out of this thing."

"Well, I can't just change in front an open window… Is there a bathroom?"

"There's one in the back, but it's a little rough. I live upstairs. You're welcome to use mine. I'll just leave the door unlocked and you can come up whenever you need anything."

Amelia sat on the edge of the bed. "I'm sure I'll be fine. And I don't want to keep you from work. I know you're a very busy man around town."

"No," he said. "Not so busy."

She stood. "Well, then, maybe you can keep an eye on the bed while I go out and pick up a few things? I would really appreciate the help. And I don't trust Sam Blackstone."

Benny looked vaguely disappointed but he shrugged. "Sure. I'll be around for the next hour or two."

"You won't let Sam take the bed?"

"Nope," Benny said. "I'm your man. You can count on me…Amelia."

She grabbed her purse and headed for the front door, grateful to make her escape. Given time, maybe Benny could be convinced to transfer his loyalties to a new friend. There was nothing to stop her pleading her case to him. That wouldn't be dishonest, would it?

She headed to the inn to gather up her things. Then she'd have to stop by the local discount store for new bedding and pillows and something to keep her fed. Amelia was willing to give the strategy a few days, and if Sam didn't relent, she'd come up with a new plan.

When she stepped inside the Blackstone, she found Sarah sitting at the front desk.

"Hello," Sarah said.

"Is he here?"

"Sam? He raced in and out about ten minutes ago. What's going on?"

"The second battle of the bed," Amelia said.

"Don't expect him to surrender. If you take on Sam Blackstone, prepare yourself for a long siege. He can be very stubborn."

"It's just a bed," Amelia said.

"I know," Sarah replied. "It's not that valuable and he's never seemed attached to it in the past. I mean, it was a gimmick to bring guests to the inn. But he seems to be obsessed with it now." Sarah paused. "Or maybe it's you he's obsessed with and not the bed." She cupped her chin in her hand and smiled at Amelia. "This really will be fun to watch."

Amelia sighed softly. "So I suppose I don't need to ask whose side you're on?"

"Oh, I'm rooting for you," Sarah said. She came out from behind the counter. "Is there anything I can do to help?"

"You could wrap up one of those pies of yours. And

I could use a couple of pillows and some sheets for the bed. And some comfortable clothes to wear. I didn't intend to spend more than a night here."

"I'll put together a little survival kit," Sarah said. "Why don't you go pack your things and I'll have them ready when you come down?"

Amelia trudged up the stairs and headed to her room at the end of the hall. When she'd left Boston, she'd expected to be less than a day. She'd expected to show her letter from Abigail Farnsworth, pick up the bed and haul it back to the city. But now that simple task had turned monumentally complex and all because of Sam Blackstone.

She unlocked her room and stepped inside. Crossing to the bed, she flopped facedown across the handmade quilt.

Maybe she ought to just give up and go home. The thought of spending a few more days with Sam was beginning to frighten her. He already had such a powerful effect on her emotions—and on her body.

Never in her life had a man held that kind of power over her. Though she tried to stop thinking about him, tried to keep her body from reacting to his touch, it was no use. And when they weren't together, Amelia had to stop herself from getting caught up in some silly fantasy. And the fantasies were only becoming more vivid as time progressed.

At first she'd imagined him kissing and touching her, and that wild, exhilarating feeling when he pulled her into his arms. But now she'd moved on to naked bodies and soft beds, whispered urges and orgasms that seemed to last forever.

Amelia rolled onto her back and pulled the pillow over her head. Her professional reputation was on the line here. She'd come to Millhaven for one thing: to get the Washington bed that she'd been promised. And suddenly that goal had become twisted up in this game with an impossibly handsome and sexy man.

Every instinct she possessed told her to give up and go home to Boston. She could make the exhibit work without the bed. Grabbing the pillow, she tossed it across the room. It hit a small tea table that sat beneath the window and something clattered to the floor.

Amelia crawled off the bed and retrieved the silver tankard that had held a small bunch of flowers and some water. The tankard looked old; clearly a rip-off of a Revere design and burnished by a believable patina. She flipped it over, searching for the maker's mark. Her gaze came to rest on a familiar set of letters: P REVERE.

Revere silver had been reproduced many times over the years and was often marked with the original hallmark. It was impossible to tell if the tankard was a true Revere.

The weight felt right for silver and the patina looked authentic. What were the chances that the Blackstone family owned some original Revere silver?

"Pretty good," Amelia murmured. She took a couple quick photos of the tankard and the hallmark with her phone and sent them to Lincoln Farraday, the museum's expert in silver and porcelain. She placed the tankard back on the table and headed for the door.

When she walked downstairs, Sarah was waiting for her, a large wicker basket dangling from her arm and two down pillows resting on a nearby chair. "I put some brownies and cookies in there, too," she said. "And a couple of menus from the restaurants in town that deliver. And a box of condoms." She smiled apologetically. "It pays to be prepared."

"Nothing is going to happen," Amelia said.

"Has he kissed you yet?"

"Yes."

"You don't know my brother. There haven't been many women in his life, but when he finds someone he likes, nothing gets in his way."

"And you don't know me," Amelia said. "I'm pretty determined myself."

"Did you see the tankard full of flowers in your room? He picked those flowers for you," Sarah said.

"And where did he get the tankard?"

"We have whole cabinets full of old silver. I stopped trying to keep it polished years ago. We use glass vases instead."

Amelia walked to the front door and Sarah held it open for her, the pillows clutched in her arms. "If I survive the night, I'd like to see the silver collection."

Sarah shrugged and waved Amelia out the door.

As she hurried to her truck, a shiver skittered through her as she thought about sleeping in the same bed with Sam.

Then she remembered her words to Sarah. She

didn't have to sleep with him. She didn't even have to let him into the building. This was a battle of wills and he had no idea how stubborn she could be.

3

SAM PULLED HIS truck up in front of Benny's Antiques and Auction Gallery and shut off the engine. Several minor crises at the inn had kept him from returning until the evening. The sun had set an hour before and the lights inside revealed the bed and its lone occupant.

Amelia sat in the center of the bed, books and papers spread out around her. She'd made a comfortable spot for herself with bedside tables and lamps, most likely provided by Benny. She wore glasses with dark rims that stood out against her pale skin. Her hair was pulled back, revealing the full beauty of her profile.

Sam watched as a pair of pedestrians strolled by the window, then backtracked to peer at Amelia. After a few seconds Amelia noticed them and gave them a little wave before they moved on. He chuckled softly. She was a beautiful but very stubborn woman—a difficult combination and one that fascinated him more and more with every moment he spent with her.

He grabbed the pizza box and six-pack of beer from

the passenger seat, then hopped out of the pickup. When he reached Benny's door, he found it locked, so he walked to the window and rapped on the glass. She glanced up and their eyes locked for a long moment. A groan slipped from his throat and his pulse quickened.

Sam pointed to the door and Amelia shook her head, turning her attention back to the book. Undeterred, he rapped on the glass again, this time holding up the pizza and beer. She shook her head again. Sam had no intention of letting her win this battle.

He set the pizza and beer on the sidewalk, shrugged out of his jacket and slowly began to unbutton his shirt. He was nearly finished by the time she looked up. Amelia scrambled off the bed and hurried to the window.

"What do you think you're doing?" she shouted, her words muffled through the glass.

"Let me in," he said. "I brought dinner."

"I'm not hungry," she said, shaking her head.

"It's cold out here," he said, rubbing his chest.

"Put your jacket on."

"Let me in."

Sam saw the indecision in her gaze. Finally she mouthed a curse and headed to the front door. He grabbed his jacket and the dinner and reached the entrance just as the lock clicked open.

Sam slipped inside and followed her into the makeshift bedroom. The bed had been made with bedding he recognized from the inn. One of the Blackstone's picnic baskets sat at the foot of the bed, along with her overnight bag. Confirming his suspicions that Sarah was a traitor, Amelia was wearing a sweater that looked like one of his sister's thrift-shop finds.

"Where have you been?" she asked. "I didn't expect you to leave me alone with the bed for so long."

"I trust you. Besides, you could never get this bed apart and loaded before someone called me."

"I'll find someone to help me…like Benny. I'm sure he could be persuaded."

"If Benny could be persuaded, you'd be halfway to Boston by now." Sam dropped his jacket on the floor and circled the bed, setting the pizza down in the center. "I brought dinner. I thought you might be hungry."

Amelia shook her head. "I can't believe we're doing this. Isn't there some way we could work this out?"

"I'm willing to entertain offers." He opened a beer, helped himself to a slice of pizza and leaned back into the pillows, stretching his legs out in front of him.

"Get your dirty shoes off my bed!" she cried.

He grinned. "My bed. And if I'm not mistaken, also my quilt and my pillows." He slid the pizza toward her with his foot. "Have a slice."

"I'm not that hungry," she murmured.

"Come on, Amelia. Let's just call a truce for tonight and enjoy some dinner." He grabbed a beer and opened it, then handed it to her. "Go on. Relax."

"I don't drink beer," she said.

"Yeah, I kind of figured that. You seem like a wine kind of girl."

"And you didn't bring me wine?"

"Bringing aid and comfort to the enemy? I'm not that stupid," he said with a laugh.

She growled in frustration and grabbed the beer from his hand. "You think you're so charming."

"I am charming."

"Then why aren't you married? Or engaged? You don't even have a girlfriend."

"How do you know that?"

"You wouldn't be here with me if you did," she said. Her voice grew soft. "You wouldn't have kissed me."

"No," he murmured. "I wouldn't do anything that would hurt you." Sam grinned. "I kinda like you, Amelia. Haven't you figured that out?"

"You brought me dinner. I guess that's a start."

"Yes, it is. So why don't you just relax and tell me all the details of your life. I want to get to know you a little better."

"Don't you think that will give you some kind of advantage?"

Sam thought about her objection, then shrugged. "All right, I'll tell you everything I already know about you and you can just fill in any holes." He took a sip of his beer. "You were kidnapped as a baby and were raised by a pair of wolves on an island off the coast of Maine. When missionaries found you in the woods, they sent you to a vocational school where they taught you how to color within the lines and how to weld. You graduated high school at the age of thirteen and then studied carpet weaving at an ashram in New Delhi. After that you—"

"All right. Ask me a question."

"Tell me about your family," he said.

She sighed. "I'm an only child. My father is a

banker and my mother does charity work. I grew up in Boston, went to private schools and then a girls' boarding school. I majored in art history in college and took a job at the Mapother a year after I graduated. I was promoted to assistant curator of special exhibitions last year."

"So, if you get this bed, what will that mean for you at work?"

She shrugged. "Nothing, really." She took a ragged breath. "They won't fire me if I don't get it."

"They won't?"

"I'm a Gardner. My mother is, anyway."

"Flowers or vegetables?"

She was in the middle of taking a sip of beer when she laughed, spitting beer on herself. Her laughter was infectious and her eyes began to water as he chuckled. "Am I missing something?"

"No," she said, gasping for breath. "It's just...charming that you thought I meant gardening. My mother's family name is Gardner. It's a very important name in Boston. Comes along with a lot of expectations."

"Such as?"

"I'm expected to find a proper husband with a large fortune and impeccable breeding. They'd already picked someone for me. We started dating when I was seventeen and we were engaged my third year of college, but then I broke it off."

"Your parents picked a husband for you?"

She shook her head. "I've known him all my life. And we've always been aware that our parents wanted us to marry. It's not quite as shocking as it sounds."

"You get a husband, I get an inn," he said. "We're kind of in the same boat. I really didn't have much choice in the matter. At least you got away."

She took another sip of her beer. "You never really get away," Amelia said. "My parents still expect me to come to my senses and marry Edward someday. After I grow bored with this silly career I've chosen and realize I do want a confining life the exact replica of my mother's."

"Who's Edward?"

"Edward Ardmore Reed. My former fiancé."

"Do you love him?" Sam asked.

Amelia groaned and fell back onto the pillows. "I should. He's a really nice guy. He's smart and kind and very patient with me. And I'm sure if we got married, I'd come to love him. But there's just no…spark." She clapped her hands over her eyes. "That sounds like such a cliché, but doesn't there need to be a spark?" She peered at him through her fingers, then pulled her hands away.

"Yes," Sam said, rolling onto his stomach. "A spark is important." His gaze met hers and for a long moment he considered how he wanted to kiss her. Soft and slow? Or fast and fiery? But in the end she pushed forward on her elbows and kissed him.

Her lips were warm, her tongue sweet and intoxicating.

Sam slipped his hand around her nape, pulling her closer, deepening their connection until he was desperate for more.

Sam brushed aside the pizza box and pulled her

body beneath his, running his hand along the length of her thigh and dragging it over his hip. He felt like a teenager, as if every sensation racing through his body was brand-new and never experienced before.

He moved his hand under the soft cotton of her sweater, exploring the silky skin beneath. When they finally paused to take a breath, their gazes met and a tiny smile curled the corners of her mouth.

"A spark," she whispered.

"That's what I'd call it," Sam said, brushing a strand of hair from her eyes. "A definite spark."

"What should we do? Throw water on it?"

"Let it burn?"

Amelia sat up with a gasp, staring out the window. Sam pushed up on his elbow. A small crowd had gathered outside, watching as if the show had been created just for them. A camera flashed and Amelia scrambled to turn off the two bedside lamps.

Sam stepped up to the window. He recognized a few faces in the crowd and shook his head. "Don't you all have something better to do with your time?" he shouted. He pounded on the window with his fist and they scattered in different directions.

When he turned around, she was standing in the shadows, clutching a pillow to her chest as if it might protect her from the curious crowd. She looked so shocked, so vulnerable, that he immediately crossed the room and pulled her into his embrace.

"I guess we sort of forgot where we were," he said.

She nodded. "Maybe you should go."

"And leave you alone in my bed?" Sam shook his

head. "Here's the deal. If you stay tonight, I stay. But if you agree to come back to the inn with me tomorrow, I'll agree to leave the bed here. I won't do anything to…repossess it."

She looked up, her gaze scanning his features for the truth in his words.

In truth, Sam didn't really care where he spent the night as long as it was with Amelia.

AMELIA DIDN'T WANT to give up her single advantage in the battle: her tenacity. It had helped her escape her parents' control, it had gotten her the job at the museum and it would get her the Washington bed! She could stay in the dusty old store overnight for one night or ten. And she would, until Sam surrendered.

But first, a little privacy was in order. He helped her find an old tarp to cover the front window and they hung it from a pair of rusty nails they'd found in the wood above the window. Once that was done, Amelia crawled into the bed and pulled the covers up to her chin, satisfied that she had enough privacy to sleep. "Good night," she murmured.

Closing her eyes, she waited, wondering what his next move would be. Would he join her in the bed? Would he try to touch her again? Amelia's pulse quickened when the mattress beside her moved and a long sigh slipped from her lips.

She opened her eyes and found him stretched out beside her, arms crossed over his chest. "What are you doing?"

"I'm sleeping in my bed," he said.

"You might have asked if it was all right with me," she said.

"Polite, but not necessary. It's my bed." He rolled onto his side and threw his arm across her waist. "We could spend the night arguing over ownership or we could find something else to do."

"We could sleep," she said.

"I'm not tired."

"What do you suggest?"

"I don't know. Maybe we could kiss? That would pass the time."

She smiled up into his sleepy gaze. She couldn't deny that she wanted to kiss Sam. It had almost become a required activity for her. She loved the way it made her feel all crazy and tingly inside. But there were other more interesting things they might try; things she'd been fantasizing about.

But Amelia had never had the courage to turn her fantasies into reality. She'd spent her entire relationship with Edward waiting for him to stumble upon something more exciting and passionate in the bedroom— and he never had.

She had a chance now to change all of that. To push past her insecurities and inhibitions to try something daring and new. "Just one kiss," she whispered.

He cupped her cheek with his hand and gently tugged her into his embrace. Amelia wasn't ready for her reaction. Her body seemed to melt against his and warmth flooded through her veins. Though he held the power to seduce her, she wasn't afraid. In truth, she'd already decided that it was exactly what she needed.

How often did a woman get a chance like this, finding a man who could arouse passions that she didn't even know she possessed? Whether she and Sam had a few days or a lifetime together, the risk of letting this experience pass her by was just as dangerous.

One perfect memory of a perfect man. That's all she really wanted. And if her life went on without him, she could survive on the memories. Maybe there would be other men, and maybe they'd steal her heart in the same way Sam had. But she'd know that she could have a relationship on her terms, one that she controlled, that satisfied her wants and desires. And right now she wanted Sam.

As the kiss deepened, Sam pushed her back into the down pillows. The weight of his body against hers caused a blissful feeling to overwhelm her and Amelia wrapped her arms around his neck and moaned softly. She'd never thought much about the pleasures of kissing. With Edward, kissing was a greeting, a farewell and a short invitation to sex. But Sam took the activity to another level.

He seduced her with his lips and his tongue, teasing and testing. And when she arched against him, he moved lower, kissing her neck and then tugging at the sweater until he exposed her shoulder. His lips traced a warm path over her skin, sending delicious sensations racing through her body.

Amelia slipped her fingers through his hair and wriggled beneath him until their bodies fit against each other. Hips to hips, legs tangled, her breasts pressed flat beneath the weight of his chest. He caught her hands and held them above her head as he nuzzled her neck.

"I know what you're trying to do," he whispered.

"You do? Would you like to tell me? I really want to get this right," Amelia said.

He pulled back, meeting her gaze with a smile. "You have no idea how beautiful you are, do you?" Sam dropped a kiss on her lips. "Not a clue."

"I wouldn't go that far," Amelia said. "My mother always used to say that grace and confidence were always more important than beauty. So, I kind of knew from an early age that I wasn't a ravishing beauty."

"Your mother was stupid and blind," he said.

"That's nice of you to say."

He kissed her again, his lips lingering over hers. Amelia tried to pull him back on top of her, but he grabbed her waist and rolled over, settling her legs on either side of his hips.

She could feel he was hard beneath the faded denim of his jeans, the ridge of his erection pressing against the spot between her legs. Amelia could almost imagine away the clothes they wore. How would it feel to toss aside the barriers between them and indulge in all the pleasures they could stand?

With him, she did feel beautiful. Was that all part of the fantasy? Or did he really see her differently than she saw herself?

Amelia reached down to grab the hem of her sweater, but before she could pull it over her head, Sam stopped her.

"Don't," he said.

Amelia stared at him for a long moment, trying to read his expression. "I...I thought you—"

"If you take your clothes off, then I'm going to want to take my clothes off and then all sorts of things are going to happen."

"And that would be a bad thing?" Amelia asked.

He braced his hands behind him and sat up. "I'm afraid it would give you an advantage," Sam said, a grin twitching his mouth.

"An advantage?"

"Yes. I'd probably want to please you in any way that I could. Then you'd ask for the bed and I'd feel compelled to give it to you."

"You think I'm trying to seduce you so you'll give me the bed?"

"Aren't you?" Sam asked.

"No!" she cried. Amelia scrambled out of the bed, pulling a pillow along with her as if it might provide some protection from his accusations. "I wouldn't do something like that. You might, but I wouldn't." She had considered it but eliminated the possibility when she realized that it wasn't who she wanted to be.

Amelia inhaled a ragged breath. "It probably wouldn't even work," she murmured.

"What?"

"Seducing you," she said. "Me seducing you."

His eyebrow arched as he watched her. "No? Why not?"

"I just wouldn't be very good at it. I wouldn't know what to do. I...I've never really seduced a man before."

He rolled onto his side and braced his arm beneath

his head. "I'm not so sure. I think if you just stood there and tried to *look* sexy, that would probably get the majority of men a little hot. Of course, if you got rid of the pillow and took off your clothes, it would be a done deal."

With a frustrated growl, Amelia threw the pillow at his head. It hit him squarely in the face. Then she stepped to the side of the bed and pulled back the covers. "Get out of my bed," she ordered.

"My bed."

"Our bed."

"The bed," he finally said with a chuckle.

"Get out of *the* bed. I don't want you to sleep here."

"You don't have a choice," Sam said. "I'm not going to leave you alone here now." He patted the mattress. "Now, get back into bed."

This was ridiculous. She was fighting her attraction to him and he was playing some silly game with her. The last thing she was thinking about when she kissed him was the ownership of the bed beneath them. In truth, the bed was becoming far less important to her than the man in it.

Amelia pulled the covers over her body, hugging the edge of the bed, her back to him. A few seconds later Sam switched off the lamp on the other side of the bed, throwing them both into darkness. She took a ragged breath before she turned her face into the pillow.

Go to sleep, Amelia, she silently ordered. *And when you wake up, everything will be all right again.*

She touched her lips with her fingertips and bit

back a groan. Now, if she could just get him to stop kissing her, she might believe it.

HER BODY WAS warm against his, her soft curves fitting his shape as if the fates had designed her only for him. Sam slipped his arm around her waist and gently pulled her closer, her backside tucked into his lap, his chin resting on her shoulder.

He hadn't known her intimately, at least not yet, but he was sure that if it ever happened, it would be amazing. His thoughts wandered back to the previous night, to the moment she'd reached down to remove her sweater. Sam hadn't expected her to make such a bold move. And his first impulse had been to let her take the lead.

But when they finally did surrender to their desires, he wanted to do it without any agendas standing between them. He didn't want their encounter ruined because of the ownership of some silly bed.

Sam took a deep breath, the scent of her hair teasing at his nose. He ought to just give her the damn bed. But Sam knew that as soon as he did, she'd pack her trailer and drive out of his life. He needed more time with her—time to figure out what this all meant.

There was definitely an attraction between them. Sexual, yes. But more than that. He could spend hours just watching her, deciphering every expression that crossed her face, cataloging all the features that combined to make her beautiful. She challenged him, made him see himself and his life in a different way. She understood him.

He pressed his lips to her neck. Memorizing the scent of her so that he might recall it at will.

She stirred slightly and Sam held his breath, wondering what she'd say if she woke with his arms around her. He heard her take a sharp breath as her slender body jerked. Then she slowly turned in his arms until she faced him.

She stared at him and he waited until she was fully awake before speaking. "Morning," Sam murmured.

"Is it morning?"

"I think so."

"I slept so well. Like a rock." She fought a yawn. "I'm not sure I moved all night long. It must be this bed."

He wanted to suggest it had more to do with her bedmate than the bed. But he needed more than one night to prove that. And a different bed. "It must be."

Sam bent closer and brushed a kiss across her lips. He heard the breath catch in her throat, then waited again to see what she might do.

A few seconds later her soft lips met his.

This time Sam did nothing to control himself; her kiss was his invitation to take more. He pulled her on top of him, smoothing his hands over her body as their hips came together. Though she still wore the sweater and yoga pants she'd worn last night, Sam had discarded his jeans and shirt, leaving just a pair of boxer briefs to cover his body.

"What happened to your clothes?" she asked.

"I can't sleep with clothes on. With anything on."

Her eyes went wide. "Are you—"

"Naked?"

"Are you?" she asked.

"Not yet," he said. "What about you? How do you usually sleep?"

"Flannel pajamas," she said. "Even in the summer. Except when I travel. Then I wear this."

"Have you ever tried naked?" Sam asked.

Amelia shook her head. "I get cold."

Sam smoothed his hands across her back, then slipped his palms beneath her sweater. His touch met warm, silken skin. "You'll be liberated. I promise."

She watched him warily, slowly shaking her head. "Why was this forbidden last night and it's all right today? I don't understand."

He pulled her down to kiss him. It was deep and delicious and slightly desperate.

"This isn't about the bed," she said, as if she sensed his doubts about her motives.

"I know," he said.

She shifted above him, the soft spot between her legs pressed against his growing erection. Sam groaned inwardly. It was going to be difficult to stop once they started. Was he ready to call an end to their battle?

Once they got physical, would it be possible to deny her anything? Could he really deny her the one thing she wanted, even if it meant she left immediately afterward?

This time when she reached for the hem of her sweater, he watched her tug it off over her head. Her hair fell in soft waves around her face and Sam reached up, brushing a strand of hair from her beautiful eyes.

His gaze drifted down, from her sleepy eyes to her

damp lips and slender neck. Below that, he found new territory, silken skin exposed for the first time. Sam smoothed his palm along the ridge of her collarbone.

His lips followed the path of his fingers, moving lower until his mouth hovered over the pink tip of her breast.

Amelia held her breath and, when he drew her nipple into his mouth, exhaled a long sigh and wrapped her arms around his neck.

"What's that sound?" Amelia whispered.

"I'm pretty sure that's the blood rushing to my lap," he joked.

"No, listen. It sounds like someone left a radio on. People talking."

He pulled back and looked up at her. Amelia's brow was furrowed with suspicion and she glanced around. When she glanced over her shoulder, Sam felt her body stiffen. An instant later she screamed, grabbed the sheet and pulled it over her head.

"What's wrong?" Sam asked, pushing up on his elbows.

He didn't need an answer. He sat straighter and stared out the front window. The tarp had fallen to one side, giving everyone gathered on the sidewalk a perfect view of what was going on in George Washington's bed.

A small crowd stood on the other side of the glass and several people held up their phones as they snapped photos of the scene. Amelia was burrowed beneath the covers beside him and Sam tugged at the covers, pulling them over his bare chest.

"Do something!" she shouted. "Don't just sit there!"

"I can't get up at the moment," he said, certain that his desire would be evident through the fabric of his boxers.

She shoved a pillow out from beneath the sheet. "Use this."

Groaning, Sam placed the pillow in his lap and slipped out of bed. The cameras began to flash and he pasted a smile on his face. He grabbed the corner of the tarp and held it up to cover the window.

"Okay," he said. "It's safe now. Get out of bed and grab your stuff. I'll hold up the tarp until you're done."

She peeked out, and when Amelia was satisfied that it was safe, she scrambled out of bed and frantically collected her belongings.

"Grab my stuff, too," Sam said. "When I let go of this, I'll need to make a run for it. They have cameras."

She picked up her pace, cursing beneath her breath. When she was finally finished, he followed her to the dark shadows beyond the plate-glass window. He watched as she quickly slipped into her sweater, his fingers twitching as he remembered the feel of her flesh in his hands.

"Mornin'." Benny Barnes appeared in the doorway of his office, a wide smile on his face. "I was wonderin' when you'd be up." His attention was fixed firmly on Amelia. "I have breakfast for you. I bought some of that French roast coffee and some nice jelly-filled dough-nuts. Can I get you some?"

Amelia glanced over at Sam and he shrugged. "I want a cold shower," he muttered.

"Shower's at the top of the stairs and to the left," Benny said, his gaze still fixed on Amelia. "Come on in, Amelia. I'll get you a cup of coffee."

"Actually, I'd like to wash my face and get dressed."

"I'll take a cup of coffee," Sam said. He turned to Amelia. "You go ahead. I'll wait down here."

He and Benny watched as she headed toward the stairs. "She's a beaut," Benny said. "You think she likes meat loaf? They got a great meat loaf special today at Addie's Café. I never miss their meat loaf."

Sam grabbed his jeans from the pile Amelia had dropped on the floor and tugged them over his boxers. "I think she has a fiancé," he said. "Some guy back in Boston."

"Hmm." Buddy frowned. "And you're not worried about sleeping with her?"

"That was all business," Sam said. He grabbed his shirt and tugged it over his head. "I want you to help me break the bed down and put it in Amelia's trailer."

"You're giving up?" Benny asked.

"Not exactly. But we can't stay here. It's too…public."

"We just have to fix that tarp," Benny said. "The nail on the right corner just popped right out and—"

"You pulled it down, didn't you?" Sam said.

Benny shrugged. "Maybe. Can't blame me for wanting to bring a little attention to my business."

Sam shook his head. "Well, everyone on that sidewalk got an eyeful this morning." He walked back to the window and found his shoes tucked beneath the edge of the bed. There were still a few people on the sidewalk, including Minerva Threadwell and her camera.

"You can go home now, Minerva," Sam shouted. "There's nothing left to see."

She gave him a thumbs-up.

Sam sat on the edge of the bed and put on his shoes, then began to yank the sheets and pillows off and tossed them on the floor. There was no way he was going to spend another minute exposed to the public view.

"Where you planning to move it to?" Benny said.

"Back to the inn," Sam said.

"You can't do that," Benny said.

"We have joint custody of this damn thing," Sam said. "As long as Amelia agrees, then there won't be a problem. And she'll agree."

By the time she came back downstairs, Sam and Benny had the bed pulled apart.

Amelia frowned. "What are you doing?"

"We're taking the bed to the inn," Sam said. "We can't leave it here."

After a long moment she nodded. "You're right. But this doesn't mean I'm giving up."

Sam grinned. "I wouldn't expect you to."

He wanted to yank her into his arms and kiss her, but he held his impulses in check. He had a plan for the bed—and the two of them—that would satisfy them both. Sam just wasn't sure for how long.

4

"WHAT IS THIS PLACE?" Amelia asked, setting her overnight bag down in the small stone structure next to the inn.

"It was the kitchen before the kitchen was in the house," Sam explained. "We use it as a guesthouse in the summer, but it only has the fireplace for heat, so it's empty for most of the rest of the year. Families like it. The inn doesn't have a lot of space for kids. And it's…private."

Amelia wandered over to the huge hearth that dominated one wall of the fieldstone cottage. Before the advent of sprinkler systems and fire hydrants, the kitchens of Colonial homes, especially inns, were housed in separate buildings to prevent fires in the main living areas.

"This was the first building built on the property," Sam said. "The bathroom is through that door. And there's a small kitchen behind that wall." He bent over the hearth and lit the kindling that he'd laid in the hearth. Flames consumed the wadded newspaper and then began to crackle around the dry sticks. "If you could keep an eye on this, I'm going to check in with Sarah. I had 9-1-1 on my phone this morning. We'll unload the bed and set it up later." Sam slowly stood and wiped his hands on his jeans. "I'll be right back."

"Could you bring some coffee?" Amelia asked.

"I'll do better. I'll bring you breakfast." He leaned closer and brushed a kiss across her cheek. But as he stepped away, his gaze fixed on her lips. In the space of a heartbeat, he pulled her into his arms and covered her mouth with his.

She should have known the nuances of his kisses by now, but each time their lips touched it was a powerful and unique experience. With this one, he didn't just press his mouth to hers or tantalize her with his tongue. This kiss was a full-on seduction, with ebbs and flows, peaks and valleys, designed to send her heart racing and her mind spinning.

As with their earlier encounters, Amelia was left wondering what awaited her beyond a kiss. She'd had a taste this morning when she'd pulled off her sweater. A shiver skittered through her as she recalled the sensation of his hands against her bare skin. If she had a choice in the matter, when he returned they'd pick up exactly where they'd left off.

"I'll be back in a few minutes," he murmured. "Why don't you make yourself comfortable?"

He walked out and Amelia sat on the edge of a chair, watching the fire grow on the grate. She walked across the room and added a few larger logs to the fire, then moved to the door.

Her SUV was parked just outside with the keys still in the ignition. Her gaze darted to her bag, sitting nearby. There was nothing to stop her from leaving. She'd be back in Boston with the bed before sundown. It would be safely inside the Mapother with its alarms and steel gate and there'd be nothing he could do.

She'd stopped herself from leaving earlier because she wanted to live her life truthfully, no pretending and no manipulation. But wasn't she just sitting and waiting for someone to make decisions for her again? What was more important? Honesty or winning on her own terms?

Amelia took a shaky breath and reached down for her luggage. She chose to win.

She walked to the door and stepped outside. Her heart pounded so loud, Amelia was sure she could hear it echoing through the leafless trees. She hurried around to the driver's side and tossed her bags onto the backseat, then slipped behind the wheel.

She started the Lexus, wincing when the engine roared, and threw the SUV into gear. Thankfully Sam had backed the trailer up to the door, so she had a straight shot out of the driveway and onto the road.

By the time she reached the outskirts of town, she felt the first pangs of guilt. She didn't want to leave, but Amelia knew that her motives had changed considerably since she'd arrived in town.

At first, all she'd cared about was the Washington bed. But over the past few days she'd nearly forgotten her original purpose. She'd been caught up in this crazy infatuation that seemed to grow more powerful with each minute she spent with Sam.

The truth was that she'd never expected to feel this way about a man. She'd watched the rather cool relationship between her parents as she'd grown up and considered that the norm. And then with Edward, there had always been a distance between them. Though they knew each other well, they'd each kept a part of themselves away, behind the cover of propriety. Though their relationship had felt safe, it had never felt particularly complete.

Edward rarely teased her or joked around. He didn't look at her as if he might devour her at any moment. And sex was…perfunctory.

"Perfunctory," Amelia muttered. She knew the meaning of the word, but she'd never admitted that it perfectly summed up her sex life with Edward.

She couldn't remember a time when he'd just grab her and kiss her for no reason. Or laughed out loud at something she said. The things she found amusing, he found odd. The things she found interesting, he found insignificant. She'd nearly settled for a marriage that would have been nothing more than a legal agreement with a very bland man.

"Bland man," Amelia said, laughing softly. Why were all these things suddenly occurring to her now? When she'd left Edward, it hadn't been to find some grand passion. She'd expected to be satisfied with her career…until Sam had stumbled into her life. Or rather, she'd stumbled into his.

They made absolutely no sense together and yet he

made her laugh. Such a simple thing, but it was something she couldn't imagine living without.

He also made her heart race and her pulse pound. When he touched her, she seemed to melt inside, the heat pooling in very specific spots. Amelia wanted to know how it would feel when he finally touched her everywhere.

She reminded herself that desire was just another form of control. And she wasn't sure she was strong enough to break that bond twice.

By the time she was ready to put the subject of sex with Sam aside, Amelia was thirty miles out of Millhaven, ready to hop on the I-90 to Boston. The guilt she'd felt earlier was gone, leaving her with the uneasy feeling that rationalizing her actions came quicker than expected.

The bed was hers. She had no question on that matter. Abigail had given it to the museum. And for all she knew, Sam's claim to the bed was bogus. Why would Abigail agree to buy the bed and then just give it back later?

Still, he'd trusted her and she'd betrayed him at the first available opportunity. Though they had battled over the bed, he didn't deserve that. Maybe she should have waited until they'd come to some sort of understanding or agreement before taking off.

The sound of a siren caught her attention and she slowed, searching for the source in her rearview mirror. The patrol car was approaching at a fast speed and Amelia carefully veered onto the side, waiting for him to pass. But to her surprise, he pulled in behind her.

"Oh, my God," she murmured. Sam had called the police. He'd had her license number from when she'd registered at the inn! And she'd stolen a very valuable and historical piece of furniture. Never mind that it was technically half hers. Amelia's heart raced as she brought the SUV to a stop. Maybe there was another reason he'd pulled her over. But her registration was up-to-date and she'd made a complete stop at the entrance to the freeway. Just a routine stop, perhaps?

She glanced over at the passenger seat, searching for her purse. She panicked when it wasn't there, then realized it was on the backseat. She grabbed it.

It seemed to take hours before the highway patrolman got out of the car and approached her window. Amelia held her breath.

"License and registration," he said.

"I don't think I was speeding," Amelia said.

"License and registration," he repeated.

Amelia rummaged through her wallet and produced the required items. She decided it would be best to hold her tongue and wait for the officer to speak.

"You're from Boston?"

"Yes, sir," she said.

"What are you doing in the area?"

Did he already know? Should she be honest and admit her wrongdoing? "A little mini vacation."

"What's in the trailer?"

She took a deep breath. Either he already knew the answer to that question or he didn't. If he did, then she'd be under arrest in a matter of minutes. How was she going to get out of jail? Who could she call?

"It's an antique bed," Amelia said. She held her breath.

"Are you an antiques dealer?"

"No, I work for the Mapother Museum in Boston. I can show you my business card if you'd like."

He nodded and Amelia retrieved a card from her purse. She held her breath as he examined it, then handed it back to her.

"You have a defective taillight on your trailer," he finally said. "I'm giving you a warning but I'd advise you to pull off at the next exit and check on the connections."

"I'll do that," Amelia said. "Thank you." She took the warning ticket he held out and tucked it in her purse, a flood of relief washing over her. "Thank you. Have a lovely day."

He gave her a nod and walked back to his patrol car. Amelia watched his reflection in the driver's side mirror. Then she carefully pulled into traffic. He followed her closely for the next few miles, and when she reached the exit, Amelia turned off and he continued on down the interstate.

She parked the SUV and trailer in the lot near a filling station. Closing her eyes, she leaned back into the soft leather seat.

She was crazy to think there was anything more than simple lust between her and Sam. And her job was important. If she wanted to continue to live without help from her parents, she needed a decent income. All of which meant she had to return to Millhaven and make sure she owned the bed free and clear.

She'd come to an agreement with Sam about the bed. And they'd play out whatever crazy passion they had between them. But she wouldn't let him dictate her future.

"How many rooms do we have booked for tomorrow night?"

"Just three," Sarah said. "But we have that big wedding party coming in this weekend. Friday and Saturday night we're completely booked."

"Will James be able to install the new boiler by then?" Sam asked.

After leaving Amelia, Sam had walked into a disaster at the inn. Sometime during the early morning hours the old boiler that fed the inn's water-heating system had finally died. Though the death had been expected for at least the past fifteen or twenty years, there had never been enough money to replace it.

"James says that he can float us for his labor but we have to come up with the money for the boiler."

"How much?"

"Nine thousand. He says we need two boilers, one for each wing. I suppose we could close off one wing and save a little money, but that's not going to help us this weekend. I'll see if I can find some space heaters. And we'll get all the fireplaces going."

"How are we going to pay for this?" Sam asked, pacing back and forth in front of the desk. "My credit cards are maxed out. We've got nothing saved. And I've got a list of another ten projects that have to be done in the next year that will cost just as much."

"We could ask Daddy for another loan."

"No," Sam said. "The inn is my responsibility."

"How is this fair?" Sarah asked. "You didn't want this place. You should have just told him you weren't going to run it."

"How was I supposed to say that to him? He spent his life keeping this place going just so he could leave it to us." Sam took a deep breath. "Any ideas how we're going to pay for this?"

"We could sell something," she said. "We could have sold the George Washington bed again if you hadn't given it to Amelia."

"I didn't give it to Amelia," he said.

"Then why did she leave with the trailer about a half hour ago?"

Sam gasped. "What?"

"Yeah. I just figured you'd worked out your deal with her and she was headed back to Boston."

Sam shook his head. "We didn't have a deal. Not yet." He chuckled softly. "I guess she got the best of me. I didn't think she'd just steal the bed." Raking his hands through his hair, he cursed softly.

"You were down in the basement, looking at the boiler with Jerry. I assumed it had all been settled last night." Sarah shrugged. "Maybe she just had a few errands to run. She'll probably be back."

Sam shook his head. "No. She had no errands to run. I was going to get her breakfast and then I got distracted. She had a chance and she decided to take it."

"A chance?"

"A chance to steal the bed. She's probably halfway to Boston by now."

"I don't really understand why you're so obsessed with that silly bed. You didn't care about it when Abigail had it."

"I thought we could sell it again," Sam said.

In truth, it wasn't about the bed anymore. It was about the woman who wanted the bed. He'd already decided to give it to her. But he figured he could drag the fight out a little longer, to keep her in his life just a few days more before sending her home.

"Then go get it back from Amelia and see if you can work out a deal. But do it today. We have to get the new boiler paid for and installed in the next forty-eight hours or wedding attire will have to include down-filled jackets. No bride wants the space-heaters-and-outerwear look."

"Our electrical system won't be able to handle all those space heaters," Sam said. "We'll be blowing circuits all weekend long. And they're a fire hazard." He cursed softly. Sam hated living this way, when every day was a potential disaster just waiting to happen.

When he'd started managing the inn, business had been good for the first couple years. He'd even managed to put away a nice little nest egg he'd hoped to spend on a tropical vacation or maybe a fishing boat. But that had disappeared over the past few years, along with every ounce of credit he possessed. Bad plumbing, spotty electrical systems, a new roof, two crumbling chimneys...the list seemed endless.

"I'm going to stop at the bank and see if they'll give

us a short-term loan for the boiler. Then I'll rework the housekeeping schedule for this weekend. You and I will have to handle everything."

"Eleven rooms? I can't do that and cook."

"Then I'll do it," Sam said. "With what we make this weekend, we should be able to pay for a good bit of the boiler. After that, we've got to find a way to get more business."

Sam grabbed his keys and started toward the front door. "Call James and tell him we'll get the money. He can install the boiler tomorrow."

"What if the bank says no?"

"I'll deal with that when it happens. Just say we have the money."

Sam's truck was parked where he'd left it, in front of the old stone kitchen. He reached for the door of the pickup, then stopped himself and instead walked to the front door of the cottage. If she had left to run errands, her luggage would still be there.

He jogged up the steps and walked inside, holding his breath. "Hell," he muttered, his gaze fixed on the empty spot on the floor. She was gone.

Maybe he'd misread what was happening between them. He'd assumed that the battle for the bed was just a game they were playing, an excuse to spend more time with each other. Possession had been important at first, but Sam's priorities had changed. He cared more about Amelia's wants and needs than he did his own.

So where did he go from here? He should hop into his truck, drive to Boston and take his damn bed back. But all he really wanted back was her. Was that crazy?

He barely knew her, yet when they were together something seemed so right.

Sam crossed the room and stood at the hearth, staring down into the spent embers. The door squeaked behind him. When he turned, he expected to see Sarah with another declaration of doom. But instead he came face-to-face with the girl of his dreams.

They both stared at each other for a long moment, neither one moving. He inhaled a sharp breath, suddenly short of oxygen. Then, as if the spell were broken, he crossed the room and pulled her into his arms, his lips coming down on hers.

The kiss spun out into one long, delicious encounter of damp lips and desperate sighs, of cold hands trying to find warm skin. He slammed the door shut behind her, then pulled her toward the bed, their lips clinging together as they moved.

He didn't want to know the truth of why she'd left or why she'd returned. It didn't matter. She was here in his arms and that was enough.

"I'm sorry," she murmured. "I shouldn't have left."

"I don't care," he said, his lips hovering over hers.

"But I need to explain. It wasn't just about the bed. I got…frightened. Over what was happening between us. About the hold you have over me. And…I care about what you think of me."

"I think you're wonderful and beautiful—"

"And honest," Amelia added.

As they stood by the bed, they began to shed clothing, casting aside barriers with each item tossed to the floor. Her jacket, his shirt. Her sweater, his jeans. And when they stood in front of each other in just their underwear, Sam kissed her again, this time more gently, waiting for her to invite him into her bed.

He exhaled slowly as she picked up his hands and pulled him to the bed. They fell onto the mattress in a tangle of limbs.

Sam ran his fingers through her hair and molded her mouth to his, their kisses growing more desperate by the moment.

Amelia reached between them to unhook her bra but a frantic rapping at the door caused her to freeze. She looked up at him, her eyes wide and questioning. Were they going to ignore the knock or continue?

"Sam? Sam, are you in there?"

He cursed softly. "My sister," he murmured.

"You'd better get it."

Sam grabbed the quilt from the bed and wrapped it around her, dropping a kiss on her lips. "Stay right here."

Sam strode to the door and opened it a crack. "What do you want?"

"Something happened. There's water leaking all over the basement. I think it's coming from the water heater," she said.

"Not the boiler?"

"No. You don't have to come right away. It's just a puddle right now. But if—"

"I'll come," he said. "I'll be there in a few minutes."

He closed the door and pressed his forehead against the rough planks. He turned and walked toward Amelia, gathering his clothes along the way. "There's an emergency I've got to tend to," he said, pulling her into his arms and kissing the top of her head. "Will you wait for me this time?"

She nodded. "I'll be right here."

When he was completely dressed, Sam gently took the quilt from her, exposing her body to the cold. He worked at the clasp of her bra, then hooked his thumbs into the fabric of her panties and pulled them down over her hips.

Amelia leaned into the warmth of his body as he ran his hands over her silken skin. She shivered and he pulled her closer. "There. Now you know I'll be back."

Amelia grabbed the quilt and wrapped it around her again, then sat on a nearby chair. "I'll be waiting."

"I'll try not to be too long," Sam said.

As he walked out the door, he glanced over his shoulder at her and smiled. He'd been waiting for this moment since the second he'd set eyes on her. After she'd run away with the bed, he'd assumed it would never happen. Now she was here again and he wasn't letting a damned leaky water heater get between them.

"This place is going to drive me mad," he muttered as he strode up the drive to the inn. It was time to make some hard decisions about his life, about what he was willing to give up just to keep the family legacy alive.

"I JUST GOT a call from the *Globe*. They're running a little article and a photo in their arts section tomorrow."

"A photo?" Amelia leaned forward on the chair, pressing her cell phone more closely to her ear. "What kind of photo?"

"I don't know," Vivian said. "He mentioned something about John and Yoko. I don't really care. The *Globe* seemed fascinated by your little standoff over the George Washington bed. You can't buy publicity like this, darling. Whatever you've got going on there, don't stop. I want this story to last as long as possible. I've got our marketing department on it and I'm hoping that we can get one of the local television stations to send a news crew."

"But we moved the bed," she said. "I thought it was a little...unseemly. I mean, people were watching me sleep, and Sam agreed that we could bring it back to the inn."

"Well, take the bed back to the store," Vivian said. "I want you out there, in the public eye, selling this story. When was the last time they ran a story about the Mapother on the network news? Never."

There had to be a way to dissuade Vivian, Amelia thought. The last thing she wanted to do was to return to Benny's and sleep in that window. "There is one thing," she said. "I think I've found a piece of Revere silver."

"Where?"

"Here at the inn. I haven't had a chance to go through their collection, but one of the innkeepers told me they have cupboards full of old silver."

"All right, we'll make that priority number two. As soon as we get more press on the bed, we'll move on to the silver. This could be the luckiest week the Mapother has ever had. Keep up the good work, Amelia. I'm quite proud of you."

Amelia switched off her phone and slumped down on the chair. This was crazy. They'd just packed up the damn bed that morning. Now she'd have to haul it back and do it all over again. And she'd have to ask Sam to sleep with her. If that wasn't the most humiliating thing she'd ever done, she didn't know what was.

But she needed this job. Going back to her parents was impossible. There were some surrenders that she'd never agree to and that was one. She'd worked hard to take complete control of her life and she didn't want to give it up.

She stood up and grabbed her purse, dumping the contents out on the bed. She'd tucked the credit card in a hidden slot in her wallet and hadn't touched it in two years. Amelia pulled it out and stared down at the small piece of plastic.

Her father had given her the card on the day she'd left home, trying to convince her that she'd never be able to make it on her own. The card didn't have a limit and he'd told her to use it whenever she needed, but Amelia had refused to touch it. It was time to cut the very last tie to her old life and do what was necessary to make a success of the life she'd built.

She walked to the small kitchen on the other side of the wall. She found a pair of kitchen shears in the silverware drawer and took them out. She hesitated, then replaced the shears in the drawer. She never intended to use the card, but it was the last link she had to her father, and she wasn't quite ready to sever it just yet.

With a soft sigh she grabbed her clothes and put

them on. Sex with Sam Blackstone would have to wait. She had a bed to move, and since she'd be living in Benny's front window, she was going to make it look a lot better than it did right now. And there would be no falling tarp. A proper curtain would protect them both from prying eyes.

She pulled Benny's card out of her wallet and quickly dialed his number. "Benny, it's Amelia Sheffield. I'm going to need your help. Can we meet at your shop in about fifteen minutes?"

When their plans were finalized, Amelia stuffed everything into her purse and headed for the door. She'd get their "bedroom" set up and then she'd explain the next few days to Sam. One thing was perfectly clear: she had to convince him to give her the bed. Maybe not for keeps, but at least for the course of her President's Day exhibit. She pulled on her jacket, gathered up her luggage and tossed it into the Lexus. Thank goodness they hadn't brought the bed back inside. She carefully turned the SUV around and slowly drove out to the street.

The skies had darkened to gray and it looked as though there was snow coming. She could imagine the town covered with a glittering coat of white and smiled at the romance of it. Though she loved living in Boston, Amelia understood the appeal of small-town life. The pace was slow, the people friendly.

And then, there was the man. Though there were plenty of available guys in Boston, she hadn't managed to meet many of them. She'd come to Millhaven and met the sexiest single guy in the state of New York in her first few minutes.

Amelia smiled to herself, steering the truck down the long hill into town. He was an incredibly passionate man and, for some reason, he'd decided to turn that passion in her direction. She ought to enjoy it while she could.

A sound of a honking horn interrupted her thoughts and she glanced in her sideview mirror to see a pickup trying to pass her. Another car was approaching in the opposite direction and she pulled closer to the center line, hoping to prevent an accident.

The oncoming car passed a moment later and the pickup pulled up beside her. To her shock, she realized that it was Sam's truck and he was behind the wheel. He shouted at her but she shook her head, unable to hear what he was saying.

When they reached the bottom of the hill, Sam slowed the truck and she followed him as he pulled over to the side of the road. Amelia rolled down the window as he jumped out of the truck and strode to her.

He looked angry. "Where the hell are you going?"

"I—I'm taking the bed to Benny's," she said.

He opened his mouth, as if to shout at her, then snapped it shut. "Why would you take it to Benny's? We just moved it this morning."

"It's a long story, but my boss wants us to set it up there again. I guess we got some publicity from last night and she wants more. So, I have to ask if you'll sleep there tonight...with me..."

"Amelia, I have an inn that's falling down around

me. I have guests coming in for the weekend and we have no heat and no hot water. I've got to find a way to pay for the repairs with absolutely no money."

"I'll take care of the bed," she said. "Don't worry. It's fine if you don't sleep there tonight. Vivian will just have to deal with it."

"I have to get back to the inn. Can we talk about this later?"

"Sure," she said. Amelia paused, then reached out and touched his cheek with her fingertips. "Are you going to be all right?"

"I'm not sure," he said. "Right now, I feel as if the earth is shifting beneath my feet. I'm going to have to make some hard decisions."

"Do you want to talk about it?" she asked. "I might be able to help." She remembered the credit card in her wallet, the one her father had given her in case of emergencies. This qualified as an emergency on all counts. And she would feel no guilt in using it for someone other than herself.

He chuckled softly. "There's not much you could do about it. This is all on me." He glanced over his shoulder as a car passed them. "So…I have to get going."

"I might know people who could give you the money—"

"No," he said.

"But—"

"No," Sam repeated. "I'll figure this out. I always do. I don't need your help, Amelia, but thank you for the offer. I do appreciate it, though. I'll see you later."

He reached through the window and cupped her face

in his hands, giving her a soft but urgent kiss. "Things don't seem quite so dire when I'm kissing you."

"Ah, so I can help."

"Maybe you can," he murmured.

With that, he turned and strode back to his pickup. Amelia fought the impulse to run after him, to kiss the worry off his forehead and make him smile. She and Edward had never shared their worries or concerns with each other and she hadn't thought it a big deal. But now, a man she'd known for just three days had exposed his vulnerable side and she wanted to wrap him up in hugs.

"You are far too romantic," Amelia muttered to herself. "And that's going to get you into trouble."

Where had that romantic streak come from? Amelia wondered. It certainly wasn't genetic. And she hadn't learned it from Edward. His notion of romance was to bring her flowers every Friday afternoon—the exact same bouquet from the same florist, every week.

Amelia steered out onto the street and headed toward Benny's place. A few minutes later she pulled up in front of the storefront. Benny was standing on the front stoop, a wide smile on his face. "Didn't expect that you'd be back," he said as she walked toward him.

"Neither did I," she admitted. "This time we're going to do things a bit differently. If we're lucky, we can both benefit from this silly little game."

"Yeah?" He laughed. "Well, I like the sound of that. You just tell me what to do."

5

SAM GRABBED THE picnic basket from the front seat of his truck, then hopped out and crossed the street in front of Benny's Antiques and Auction Gallery. The lights were on inside. On the street, an elderly couple and their golden retriever stood at the window, staring at the scene inside.

He joined them, taking in the room that Amelia had created. An eclectic collection of furniture had been arranged in the window and perfectly decorated with antique linens and quilts, old crystal vases and Victorian lamps. She'd even brought in an old gramophone.

A moment later she appeared, carrying an old oil lamp. She set it on a small table draped with a lace tablecloth and set with antique china and silver.

He rapped on the window. When she saw him, she smiled and waved.

He waited as she left the window space and unlocked the front door. "Come on in," she said, stepping aside to let him pass.

"What have you done?"

"I made it look good. Vivian said there might be more media coming, so I figured I might as well up my game a little. And Benny has offered me a job doing his windows for the rest of my life, so I have that if this falls through. He also promised to marry me, but we're going to wait on that."

"It's nice," he said. "Sarah made us some dinner. I'm sorry I'm so late."

"You're here now. That's all that matters."

He slipped his arm around her waist and pulled her closer. "I want to kiss you, but those people are watching."

"Go ahead," she replied. "Give the crowd a thrill."

"All right. I'll do my best." He slipped his arms around her waist and bent her back in dramatic fashion. Then he kissed her. The sensation of his lips on hers sent a rush of desire through his body.

"How was that?" he murmured.

"Perfect," Amelia replied.

He pulled her upright, then grabbed the picnic basket and opened it. "I'm starved. Let's have some dinner."

The moment he opened the basket, the smell of food wafted into the air. He handed her a series of containers and she took them over to the table and arranged them neatly. When he withdrew a bottle of wine, Amelia smiled. "Sarah thinks of everything."

He poured them both a glass of wine and handed her a goblet. Softly touching his glass to hers, he took a deep breath. "To tonight."

"Tonight," she said.

He held out her chair for her. "Where did you find all of this?" Sam asked.

"I went digging through Benny's collection. He has two floors of antiques. He's quite the collector. And he knows his stuff. Your chair is a Burton Sawyer ladder-back. Burton Sawyer made furniture in Albany right after the Revolutionary War. His pieces can be quite valuable. And I believe this table is a Francis Harrington. He's famous for that slight curve cut in the feet."

"Benny isn't the only one who knows his stuff."

"I'm good with the furniture and textiles, but I still have a lot to learn about silver."

They enjoyed their dinner, lingering over the wine. All the tensions of Sam's day started to dissolve as he sat with her. For the first time he understood the pleasures of having a partner in life. He'd never given that aspect of a relationship much thought. His reluctance to tie another person to the anchor that was the Blackstone Inn had always been first in his mind.

But with Amelia he felt he could talk to her about almost anything and she'd listen intently and know exactly how to reply. She really was an extraordinary woman, the kind of person who could fascinate him for many years to come.

And yet it was impossible. She didn't belong here, stuck in a small town, tied to responsibilities that weren't her own. He could never do that to her.

"So what was going on at the inn this afternoon?" she asked.

"Mechanical meltdown and financial ruin," Sam

said. "Just when things start to look up, we get thrown a curveball and we're back to square one. Actually, this time, we're back to negative numbers." He sighed. "The truth is I need some quick cash, so I'm willing to let you buy the bed. I have no idea what it's worth. I trust you'll give me a fair price."

She seemed surprised at his offer. "You're ready to give up?"

"For a price. I have a plumber who has to be paid before the end of the day tomorrow."

"How much do you need?"

"At least ten thousand. But twenty thousand would be better."

"I'm sorry but your bed isn't worth more than three," she said. "And I can't buy it. We don't have the budget for that. My job is to get people to gift pieces to the museum."

He sighed. "It was worth a try," he said. Sam pushed back from the table. "So, what's the plan with this window thing? How long are we supposed to sleep here?"

"Not long," she murmured. "You said you needed ten thousand?"

Sam shook his head. He should never have brought it up. It had just felt so good to have someone to share his troubles with, but now he realized that it made him look incompetent. "I'll figure it out."

"The other day, when I was staying in the room at the end of the hall, there was a little mug on the table with flowers in it. I think it might be a Revere mug."

"Paul Revere?"

She nodded. "I'm not sure you could find a buyer

in a day, but you might be able to use it as collateral for a bank loan. I did a bit of research on the internet and one similar to it sold for thirty thousand last year. They don't come up often."

"You're telling me that we have a mug at the inn that's worth thirty thousand and it's just sitting in one of our rooms."

"With flowers in it. I'd have to have our silver curator look at it, to be sure. But I've already taken a few photos with my phone and sent them to him for his initial impressions."

Sam ran his fingers through his hair, stunned at the revelation. If she was right, then his problems were solved. Could it be that easy? "It's like you came along at the perfect time."

Amelia shrugged. "I could have slipped the mug into my bag and you never would have missed it."

"Like you tried to steal the bed this morning?" he teased.

Her smile faded. "That was not my best moment," she said. "I'm sorry about that."

Sam frowned. "I did give you the benefit of the doubt at first. I assumed you had some kind of business in town and couldn't unhitch the trailer on your own."

"No, I got all the way to the interstate before I stopped and reconsidered."

He reached across the table and grabbed her hand, pressing a kiss to it. "Why did you come back?"

"I didn't want to end it like that. In an act of dishonesty. And I didn't think we were finished yet," she said. "I guess I'm not perfect."

"I'm not, either. And we're not finished," he said. "You were right about that."

Would they ever be finished? Sam couldn't imagine reaching a point where he would be willing to let her go. Yet he knew he would have to.

Her life was in Boston. She was a city girl with dreams that could only be met in a place such as Boston or New York. Millhaven would never satisfy her. Hell, he could barely stand the small town and he'd spent his whole life here.

And yet Sam had to wonder how different he'd feel if he had someone to share his life. Would the inn still seem like an anchor or would he begin to see the possibility of finding true happiness here? She'd already changed him in tiny ways. Was Amelia capable of causing such a profound shift in his life?

He stood and wandered over to the gramophone. "Does this thing work?"

Amelia followed him, standing beside him as he peered inside. "I don't know. There are records in the cabinet. We can try it."

"A little music might be nice." He heard her shudder beside him and he turned to find her rubbing her arms. "Cold?"

"It's a little drafty in here. The wind has picked up and it seems to blow straight through that glass window." She handed him a record. "I think it's time to pull the curtains."

She walked over to the side of the display window and pulled a cord, dropping a thick velvet curtain across one half of the window.

"Guaranteed not to fall down in the middle of the night."

"Where did Benny get that?"

"It's out of the old movie theater in town," Amelia said. She pulled the other side and suddenly they were alone in a cozy room, soft lighting creating shadows on the false walls.

Sam cranked up the gramophone, then slipped the record out of the sleeve. "This is Rudy Vallee. 'If You Were the Only Girl in the World.'"

"Really?" Amelia said.

"It has a great beat and it's fun to dance to," Sam said. "I'll give it a ten."

"It's a thought-provoking title," she said.

Sam put the record on and dropped the needle at the edge. The gramophone crackled for a moment before the sounds of a saxophone drifted out of the old speakers. A few moments later a wavering voice was added. Smiling, Sam listened to the words.

When he turned around, he found her sitting on the edge of the bed, her feet dangling off the edge. She patted the spot beside her.

"You don't want to dance?" he asked.

She grabbed his hand and pulled him down to the mattress, then stood in front of him. When she reached for the top button of her sweater, Sam held his breath, his mind flashing back to earlier in the day, when he'd left her naked and alone.

He braced his hands behind him on the bed as he watched, taking in every detail as her clothes came off. Inch by inch, she revealed her pale skin. And though it was a fairly tame striptease, to him it was incredibly sexy and provocative.

When she was finally free of all her clothes, he took in the full impact of her naked body on his senses. He felt his breathing grow shallow and his pulse quicken. Heat seemed to snake through his bloodstream, setting his nerves on fire. He wanted to touch her, to pull her body into his arms and kiss her, but Sam waited.

"Now you," she murmured.

He kicked off his shoes and socks, then slowly stood in front of her. He'd never been shy about his body. He considered himself a decent-looking guy. But he wanted Amelia to see him as more than just some ordinary man. He wanted her to need him, to be obsessed with him the same way he'd become obsessed with her. Then she'd never want to leave.

He'd never made love to a woman where so much was on the line.

AMELIA TOOK IN the beauty of Sam's naked body. Until this moment her casual observations of his form had usually ended when he noticed her staring—or when her body's reaction was too much to bear. But right now Amelia didn't care that her gaze kept dropping to the more unfamiliar spots of his body.

She understood male anatomy, in theory. But Sam was only the second man she'd ever seen naked. Edward had only ever wanted to have sex in the dark, but even still it was clear that Sam was a much more… developed specimen than Edward. Sam was lean, but still muscular, with beautifully defined biceps. Her gaze drifted down to his legs, which were long and covered with a soft dusting of hair.

"How long are you going to stare at me?" he asked, a boyish smile on his lips.

"Do you have somewhere else you need to be?"

"Yeah," he said.

"And where is that?" Amelia asked.

"Inside you."

His words caused a shiver to skitter up her spine. His words took away any doubt she might have about what they'd be doing together. Amelia took a step toward him. "I've never really looked at a real naked man before. Not in great detail. I've studied all the great nudes, of course, but those are just paintings and statues. They aren't living, breathing flesh. There's a difference, you know."

She moved behind him and ran her hands across his back, her fingers stopping over a raised scar on his right shoulder. "When did you get this?" she asked, pressing a kiss to the spot.

"When I was young and stupid. I jumped off a cliff over the Hudson and hit a rock on the way down."

"Ouch," she said.

"So, what *is* the difference?" he asked. "Between a real man and art?"

"The artist wants to portray perfection—the perfect proportions of the human body. Without the scars. But he can't paint the warmth of your skin or the softness of the hair on your chest. He can't show me the scent of your skin."

He grabbed her hand and pulled her around in front

of him. "Do you always do so much talking when you're naked?"

"I've never been quite this naked before. Am I talking too much?"

He slowly shook his head, his gaze still fixed on her face. "It's all right. You can ask me anything." Sam smoothed his hand down her torso and then between her legs.

Amelia gasped as he began to caress the damp folds and the cleft beneath. A powerful tremor raced through her body and, for a moment, she thought her knees might give way beneath her. Sam seemed to know exactly what he was doing. She could only pretend at competence.

He kissed her hungrily, desperately, and she grew light-headed. With an arm around her waist, he pushed her toward the bed. The edge of the mattress hit the backs of her knees and she fell into the soft quilts, pulling him along with her.

He pinned her arms above her head and kissed a trail from her lips to her collarbone. Then, releasing his grip on her hands, Sam delved lower, finding her breast, then her nipple.

Amelia arched beneath him; a silent invitation to continue. She needed more. Her mind was filled with images—quick, fleeting—giving her just a quick taste of what he might offer her.

He seemed fascinated with her breasts, his tongue and lips drawing her nipples to hard peaks. But then his exploration continued. Anticipation surged when he gently pushed her knees apart and slid off the bed to the floor.

She knew what he was going to do, even though Amelia hadn't had much experience with this variety of seduction. Her only lover had preferred to limit lips and tongues to more conventional uses such as kissing. As his mouth finally found its destination, Amelia's body reacted instantly.

A soft cry tore from her throat and she twisted beneath him. Sam grabbed her hips, refusing to allow even a momentary retreat. The pleasure was almost too intense to bear, but Amelia tried to control her body and focus her thoughts.

She pushed up on her elbows and watched him, fascinated by his single-minded purpose. Delicious sensations pulsed through her and, before long, she closed her eyes and lay back, overcome by pleasure. Every thought was centered on the touch of his tongue.

The tension began to build inside her, driving her forward toward inevitable release. She craved that feeling of tumbling over the edge, the risk, the exhilaration and the sweet exhaustion that would follow. But she didn't want to fall just yet.

She came close again and again but forced herself to wait, rebuilding the tension until it never really went away. Then Amelia reached for him, pulling him up along her body.

Her fingers closed around his hard shaft and she stroked him, gently bringing him closer to the edge. She felt the weight of his body above her, and when she spread her legs, he sank down, his hips meeting hers.

For a moment, as the tip of his cock teased at her entrance, she considered a condom. But she'd kept up with her birth control after the breakup with Edward.

"Do we need protection?" he whispered.

She shook her head and gently guided him into her body. The sensation of him filling her, inch by inch, until he was buried deep inside her, was exquisite torture.

"Perfect," she murmured. "I knew it would be perfect."

"It gets a lot better," he murmured.

He began to move, slowly at first and then gradually building until Amelia was breathless and aching for release. When he rolled over and pulled her on top of him, she groaned, now in control of every movement they made together.

She looked down at him and smiled, certain that he was feeling every bit as much pleasure as she was. Bending close, she brushed a kiss across his lips. Sam wove his fingers through the hair at her nape and kept her lips close to his.

"Do you have any idea how much I've wanted you? You're in my head and I can't get you out."

Amelia wasn't sure what to say. The idea of people conversing during sex was a startling concept. Her head was so muddled with desire that she couldn't put a sentence together. Instead she rocked back on her knees, driving him deep inside her.

Sam slipped his fingers between them and began to caress her, and she sucked in a sharp breath, her mind suddenly clearing, her focus sharp.

Her orgasm came on quickly, building so fast that she wasn't prepared when the spasms rocked her body. A soft cry slipped from her lips as she moved above him. She had barely come down from her own release when Sam's fingers spread across her hips and stopped her from moving.

She watched him as he fought against the pleasure, but she didn't want to wait any longer. She rose up on her knees and then slowly came down on him. It was all it took to send him over the edge.

When he was completely spent, he grabbed the covers and pulled her down beside him, tucking her into the warmth of his body. "You could ask me for anything right now and I'd say yes," he murmured.

She smoothed her fingers over his brow, brushing aside his dark hair. "I think I'd be taking advantage of the situation if I asked for the bed."

"This bed is magic," he said. "I'm not sure I'd want to give it away."

"What do you think George would have to say about this?" she asked.

"I'm sure he'd approve. He was always really popular with the babes."

Amelia giggled. "He was a pretty handsome guy."

"Not as handsome as me," Sam said.

"No, not nearly as handsome as you," Amelia said, nuzzling his neck. She'd never met a man quite so handsome as Sam. And the more she got to know him, the more perfect he became.

"We're going to have to settle this disagreement over the bed at some point," Amelia said.

"Do we? I like the way it's working out right now."

"Sam, I can't stay here forever waiting for you to decide. If you're not going to give me the bed, you need to tell me."

"Maybe I haven't decided yet," he said.

"Is that true? Are you still considering giving it to the museum?"

Sam nodded. "I am."

"All right. Then I guess I can wait a little longer." Amelia smiled and snuggled closer. She could wait for the bed. But she wasn't sure how long she could live in the window of Benny Barnes Antiques and Auction Gallery. A little more privacy might be nice—especially if they planned to repeat the events of the past few hours.

And she wanted to repeat them. She needed to store up all the blissful memories for the inevitable moment when she'd have to leave Millhaven—and Sam.

SAM HEARD THE pop through the haze of sleep. Amelia was still beside him in bed, her warm body curled up against his. But Sam's instincts told him to open his eyes, and when he did, he saw Benny standing above him. He quickly glanced over at Amelia, who was sound asleep beside him. The covers were pulled up to her nose.

"What are you doing?" he whispered to Benny. "Get the hell out of here before Amelia wakes up."

"Are you two…" Benny glanced between them. "You mean, you're… Oh, my, I guess I should have knocked."

"What's that?" Sam asked, nodding at the bottle he held.

"Champagne," Benny said.

"For breakfast?"

Benny nodded. "We got a photo in the *Boston Globe* and there's a news crew from Albany outside and one from Boston on the way." The auctioneer forced a smile. "I'll just wait for you guys in my office."

Sam nodded. "I think that would be best. And don't let anyone inside until I say so, all right?"

Benny nodded, then hurried out.

Sam burrowed between the warm sheets and gently nuzzled Amelia's shoulder. She opened her eyes and smiled at him. "Tell me it's too early to get up," she murmured.

"It's too early to get up," he said.

"Tell me we're going to spend the whole day in bed," she said.

"We're going to spend the whole day in bed," he repeated.

Amelia sat up and brushed the tousled hair out of her eyes. "How do I look?" she asked.

"Beautiful," he said, dropping a kiss on her lips.

"Do I look well satisfied? Because I am, you know. I'm very well satisfied."

He reached over and smoothed a stray strand of hair out of her eyes. "Has everyone always called you Amelia?"

"Always," she said.

"You've never had a nickname?"

"No. My mother wouldn't allow it. Why do you ask?"

"Amelia sounds so formal. So proper. Nothing like the woman you really are."

She pressed a kiss to his bare chest. "My nanny used to call me Millie. I liked that name. But when my mother heard the nanny use it, she made her stop. But Nanny would still call me Millie when she was kissing me good-night. Or when I was sick."

"Can I call you Millie? That suits you so much better."

She giggled softly. "Yes, you can call me Millie." She wrapped her arms around his neck and pulled him on top of her. "Can we stop talking now?"

"I'm afraid not, Millie. There's a news crew waiting outside and Benny is just itching to talk to them. If you want to control this little story you've unleashed on the public, you're going to have to get up and make yourself presentable."

Amelia glanced over her shoulder at the covered window. "Vivian said she was going to get a crew to cover this, but I didn't think anyone would actually be interested."

"Benny said there was a picture of us in the *Boston Globe*. I guess we're news."

"I guess we are," Amelia said.

"It might be best if we make the bed before we open the curtains. I'm not sure it would be a good idea for them to find out what's really been going on in George Washington's bed."

She scrambled off the mattress and quickly began to straighten the sheets and quilts. "Help me," she said.

"Why don't you get dressed? I'll finish the bed."

She nodded and began to retrieve her clothes from the floor. When she'd finished dressing, she found her brush and dragged it through her tangled hair.

Sam watched her transform from a well-satisfied woman to a nervous wreck right before his eyes.

He smoothed his hands over the quilt and put two pillows down the center of the bed. She saw what he'd done and smiled. "Good idea."

As she put on her makeup, Sam finished dressing and picked up the copy of the *Globe* Benny had left. He stretched out on the bed and began to read it. "I'm ready," he said. "Pull the curtain and let's get this little drama on the road."

"That's a mixed metaphor," she said.

"Is that a good thing or a bad thing?" he asked.

"Just let me take the lead with the reporters. If there's anything you don't feel comfortable answering, I'll answer it. And remember, we're not supposed to like each other. We're on opposite sides of this battle over the bed."

"I'm not giving you this bed," he said. "I don't care that we've slept together or that I rocked your world. This bed is mine."

"I thought you said you were still thinking about it."

"I did and I've decided. This is my bed. At least, that's my story and I'm sticking to it."

"Fine. Play the game. And by the way, you didn't rock my world," she said.

"Yeah? You can try sticking to *that* story but I'm sure they'll be able to see the real one in your beautiful

YOUR PARTICIPATION IS REQUESTED!

Dear Reader,

Since you are a lover of our books – we would like to get to know you!

Inside you will find a short Reader's Survey. Sharing your answers with us will help our editorial staff understand who you are and what activities you enjoy.

To thank you for your participation, we would like to send you 2 books and 2 gifts – **ABSOLUTELY FREE!**

Enjoy your gifts with our appreciation,

Pam Powers

SEE INSIDE FOR READER'S SURVEY

For Your Reading Pleasure...

We'll send you 2 books and 2 gifts
ABSOLUTELY FREE
just for completing our Reader's Survey!

YOURS FREE!
*We'll send you two fabulous surprise
gifts absolutely FREE, just for trying
our books!*

Visit us at:
www.ReaderService.com

YOUR READER'S SURVEY
"THANK YOU" FREE GIFTS INCLUDE:

▶ **2 FREE books**
▶ **2 lovely surprise gifts**

PLEASE FILL IN THE CIRCLES COMPLETELY TO RESPOND

1) What type of fiction books do you enjoy reading? (Check all that apply)
- ○ Suspense/Thrillers   ○ Action/Adventure   ○ Modern-day Romances
- ○ Historical Romance   ○ Humour   ○ Paranormal Romance

2) What attracted you most to the last fiction book you purchased on impulse?
- ○ The Title   ○ The Cover   ○ The Author   ○ The Story

3) What is usually the greatest influencer when you <u>plan</u> to buy a book?
- ○ Advertising   ○ Referral   ○ Book Review

4) How often do you access the internet?
- ○ Daily   ○ Weekly   ○ Monthly   ○ Rarely or never.

5) How many NEW paperback fiction novels have you purchased in the past 3 months?
- ○ 0 - 2   ○ 3 - 6   ○ 7 or more

YES! I have completed the Reader's Survey. Please send me
the 2 FREE books and 2 FREE gifts (gifts are worth about $10) for
which I qualify. I understand that I am under no obligation to
purchase any books, as explained on the back of this card.

150 HDL GJ2A/350 HDL GJ2C

FIRST NAME	LAST NAME

ADDRESS

APT.#	CITY

STATE/PROV.	ZIP/POSTAL CODE

READER SERVICE—Here's how it works.

◀ If offer card is missing write to: Reader Service, P.O. Box 1867, Buffalo, NY 14240-1867 or visit www.ReaderService.com ▲

BUSINESS REPLY MAIL
FIRST-CLASS MAIL   PERMIT NO. 717   BUFFALO, NY

POSTAGE WILL BE PAID BY ADDRESSEE

READER SERVICE
PO BOX 1867
BUFFALO NY 14240-9952

NO POSTAGE
NECESSARY
IF MAILED
IN THE
UNITED STATES

face. Your lips are a bit swollen and you've got some beard burn on your chin. And a love bite on your neck."

"What?" She hurried over to the vanity and stared into the mirror. "Where?"

"Lower," he said.

She turned and pointed at him. "Stop it. Behave yourself or you'll be sleeping elsewhere tonight." Amelia took a deep breath, then walked to the window and pulled the curtains aside.

A small crowd had gathered and Sam noticed the news truck parked on the opposite side of the street. Within seconds, a cameraman and a reporter emerged from the van and hurried across the street.

Sam got up and walked to Benny's office. He found Benny standing at the door. "You can let them in," Sam said. "We're ready."

"You'll be sure to mention the Benny Barnes Antiques and Auction Gallery, won't you? And remember the tagline—I buy old stuff."

Sam smiled. "I'll try," he said.

"Good," Benny said. "'Cause I wouldn't want to suddenly recall what I've seen goin' on in that window…if you get my meanin'."

"Are you threatening me, Benny Barnes?"

"Nope. Just makin' a friendly request."

Benny opened the door to the shop and the reporters gladly came in from the cold. They introduced themselves and Sam led them over to the window. "This is Amelia Sheffield Gardner from the…the…"

"Mapother Museum of Decorative Arts in Boston,"

Amelia said. "And it's Amelia Gardner Sheffield. Assistant curator of Special Exhibitions."

Over the next hour the crew from Albany interviewed them both. They videotaped Sam and Amelia lying on the bed from both inside and outside the shop. Sam managed to mention Benny's name twice on camera, but to be certain the other man was satisfied, he called Benny in to answer questions about the security of the contested bed and how he was in charge of settling any small disputes that might come up between Amelia and Sam.

While they were wrapping up their first interview a second news truck arrived, this one from Boston. Sam watched as Amelia did her thing for the camera, amazed at how she hid every last trace of nerves. She looked so pretty, so self-assured. It seemed that every day there was something more remarkable he discovered about her.

When the news crew from Boston finally left, Amelia stood by the window, silently staring out at the light snow that had started to fall. She took a ragged breath and let it out slowly.

"Are you all right?" Sam asked.

Amelia nodded. "I think so."

"Did you say everything you wanted to say?"

"Yes."

"Did I say everything you wanted me to say?"

She glanced over her shoulder at him. "You were wonderful."

"Then what's wrong?"

"I just realized. My mother is going to see this. And

all her friends. My father and all his business associates. Edward."

"Edward?" Sam felt a rush of jealousy at the mention of her former fiancé. He'd never felt that way when she'd mentioned Edward in the past. But then, he'd always assumed that everything was finished between them. Now it suddenly seemed as though it wasn't. "Why would that bother you?"

"We were engaged. And the fact that his former fiancée is publicly sleeping with a man in order to win possession of a bed will be a bit hard to explain to all his friends at the club." She paused. "As for my mother, I'm sure I've broken every rule she's ever laid out for me. I suspect I'll be disowned shortly."

"Over something your boss asked you to do?"

"As far as my mother is concerned, there are no excuses for breaking her rules. And I've already broken so many of them by ending my engagement to Edward and trying to find my own career." She shook her head. "There goes my ten million."

"Ten million?"

"I have a trust fund. From my grandfather. Ten million dollars. I get it when I marry. But my parents have executive power, so they can delay giving it to me— indefinitely. It's exactly the kind of controlling game I've been trying to escape for a year."

"Wait, ten million dollars?"

Sam's mind recalled his sister's advice for solving all their problems. *Marry a woman with a ridiculous amount of money.* He'd known all along that Amelia's family was wealthy, but she'd made it clear that she'd abandoned any claim to their wealth when she'd defied their wishes.

Amelia shook her head. "It's just money," she said. "My independence means much more to me than ten million." A long silence grew between them and she crossed the room to sit beside him. Amelia slipped her arms around his waist and pulled his body against hers. "I'm sorry. That sounded so crass after all you've been through the past few days. It's just that it's not money I can spend. If I want it, I have to jump through all their hoops. So I don't even think about it anymore. It's just imaginary money."

"You get ten million and I get a run-down inn. I'd say you'll get the better end of the deal."

"No," she said. "Not at all. Believe me, it's true what they say. Money does not buy happiness."

"I would love to have enough money to test that theory. Today, I have to take that little mug over to the bank and try to convince them to give me a large enough loan to pay for the new boiler and water heater at the inn."

"I got an email from the Mapother's silver expert. After reviewing the pictures I sent, he agrees that the tankard probably is an authentic Revere, but he can't say for sure unless he looks at it. I don't think you can use it for a loan until it's been authenticated. I'm sorry." She held her breath and offered, "Let me pay for the bed."

"You said the museum didn't have the money."

"I'll buy it myself."

"You don't have that kind of money."

"I have my father's credit card."

He shook his head. "Thank you," Sam said. "I appreciate your offer. But this isn't your problem to solve, it's mine."

"Tell me," Amelia said. "When do your problems become my problems? As someone who cares about you, I want to help you with this, and I'm not sure why you think those feelings are wrong."

"I said no." His words were sharp and cold, and Sam immediately wished he could take them back. But why couldn't she understand? The last thing he wanted to do was to pull her down with him. Right now, the anchor that was the Blackstone Inn was dragging him beneath the surface and he wasn't sure he'd survive. He didn't want Amelia to suffer the same fate. She deserved more.

Sam glanced around the room. "I need to go over to the inn and check on things. I'm not sure how much time I can spend here today."

"Don't worry," she said. "I'll find something to do. Maybe I can catalog your silver collection for you. That's the first step in getting it appraised." She held up her hand. "I promise, I won't try to steal it."

"I don't know. Can I trust you?" he said, only half joking.

Amelia nodded. "You can. I promise."

"You sure you want to spend your whole day doing that?" Sam said.

"It's better than listening to Benny talk about his milk bottle collection."

Sam finally nodded. "I'll have Sarah bring some of

it over right away." He pulled her into his arms, then looked out the window to make sure no one was outside before he kissed her.

"I'll see you later this afternoon. We'll mess up that bed again."

That brought a smile to her lips and Sam felt better about leaving her. Everything was still good between the two of them. Though the outside world had intruded for a time, they were back to their little life played out in a display window.

"Be careful out there. The roads will be slippery with this snow," she said.

"You do care about me, don't you, Millie? I like that."

"And I like it when you call me Millie," she said before pulling him into one last kiss.

6

THE SNOW HAD built into a blizzard by sunset. Amelia had left the curtain pulled back so she could watch the snow fall, illuminated by the streetlights. No one was watching from the sidewalk now. No one was outside.

Earlier that day Sarah had brought her three crates of antique silver, each piece wrapped in rags yellowed with age. The final box was what had been stored in the pantry. Sarah had informed her that this was every piece of silver the Blackstone Inn owned.

Over the course of the snowy afternoon Amelia had researched the hallmarks on each item, looking them up in Benny's reference catalogs and then again with her online sources. She photographed those she couldn't find and sent the photos to Lincoln Farraday. She and Linc had started at the Mapother on the same day and they'd become great friends over the past year.

She talked to Sam a couple of times on the phone. He spent the day at the inn, helping the plumber with the installations of the new boiler and water heater. The inn was booked for the weekend and Amelia could hear the stress he was under in his voice.

She understood how he felt. The frustration, the anger that his life seemed to belong to someone—or something—else. She'd felt the very same thing near the end of her engagement to Edward. She was doing everything for her parents and nothing for herself. She was living the life they wanted for her and not her own life.

Thankfully she'd been able to walk away. Though she'd left behind a large trust fund, she'd been able to create a whole new life for herself on her own. But Sam wasn't so lucky.

Sam was tied to the inn physically as well as emotionally. He and Sarah were on call twenty-four hours a day, seven days a week. He probably hadn't taken a vacation in ages. And even if he wanted to alter his life, he couldn't. The inn would always be there; a tether to this place, this town.

She thought about the two of them together on some warm, sandy beach, palm trees rustling overhead, the ocean a beautiful turquoise blue, the days filled with sun and their nights with sex.

She tried to stop herself from getting carried away, knowing full well that there could be no future for them. They led different lives in different places. Maybe there could be a vacation here and there, though. Or a weekend away.

"Stop it," she murmured, shaking her head. She'd promised herself that she'd never let her mother control her life again. Yet here she was, planning a future with a man she barely knew. What was next? Fantasies about a diamond ring and a lavish wedding?

She didn't need a man in her life to be happy! What she needed was sex. This time with Sam had proved that. But she could get that from a casual boyfriend; a guy who came with no strings attached. A friend with benefits.

Could Sam be that man? It certainly made more sense for the two of them. A three-hour drive wasn't impossible. She made a mental note to look for a nice motel at the halfway mark between Boston and Millhaven.

But no matter what their plans, she had to return to Boston soon. Though Vivian had ordered her to remain for a bit, Amelia had responsibilities in Boston. She'd come to Millhaven on a Monday. A week away from the office was her limit, and she had to be home to help with the setup of the exhibit. The clock was ticking faster every day.

She picked up a slotted serving spoon and examined it, squinting to read the hallmark. But her mind was still on Sam.

How long could they go on as sex buddies? Was it fair to use him that way? Amelia wondered. She may not want a husband, but that didn't mean that Sam didn't want a wife. Having a partner in running the inn might make his life so much happier. If she kept him away from meeting someone like that, then she didn't really care for him at all.

And she did care for him. More than she ever thought possible. She just couldn't be his small-town girl.

"His small-town girl," she murmured, staring at the spoon. "What does that mean?"

There weren't any major museums in Millhaven or anywhere outside the big cities. But she was a smart girl. Hell, she'd managed to find something to occupy her time. She was valuing a silver collection. And after that, she had an urge to catalog all of Benny's collection and advise him on some needed divestments.

Two projects. It wasn't enough to create a career or to hold her interest for long. But if she was forced to live in a small town like Millhaven...

She'd love to completely redecorate the inn. Fresh paint and new textiles would go a long way to returning it to its former elegance. Then she'd relieve the rooms of their clutter. There were too many pictures on the walls and bric-a-brac scattered around. Simple and clean would do so much more to show off the Colonial- and Federal-style furnishings.

Then she imagined Sam's reaction.

"Oh, my," she murmured to herself, remembering how cold he'd turned after her small suggestion about paying for the bed.

As much as Sam might want a woman in his life, Amelia wondered how easy it would be for any female to fit into it. He considered the inn his own personal torch to bear, but he was very protective of the Blackstone, too. If she tried to help out at the inn, she'd have to run her every idea and action by him first. And Amelia wasn't sure she could live that way after paying such a high cost to control her own life.

They'd have to make some decisions soon about

their relationship, but none of the possibilities seemed perfectly right for the two of them. She loved her job and the independence she'd fought for in Boston. And yet she was falling in love with Sam Blackstone. No matter how she looked at the scene in her head, the two never completely meshed. If she wanted one, she'd have to let the other go.

A rap on the window interrupted her thoughts and she looked up to see Sam outside, the snow whirling around him. Amelia scrambled to her feet and hurried to the front door. She unlocked it and let him in, wincing as the cold wind and icy shards hit her face.

"It's getting nasty out there," she said.

"Six inches of snow and counting," he said, brushing the flakes from his jacket. "It's shaping up to be a huge nor'easter. Boston is completely snowed in and New York City is getting hit."

She wrapped her arms around him, brushing the cap from his head. "I'm glad I'm here," she said, pressing a kiss to his cold lips. "Snug as a bug."

"Mmm," he growled. "I'm glad you're here, too."

She helped him out of his coat and pulled him along to the window. "So, I spent the afternoon working on your silver collection."

Sam kissed her again, then grabbed the drapes and closed them, blocking their view of the snowstorm and the street. "And I've been elbow deep in mechanicals," he said, "and thinking about you the whole time."

"The whole time?" she asked.

"The whole time," he said. "Well, not every second, but certainly every minute."

"And who else were you thinking about in those other seconds?" Amelia teased. "Another woman?"

"Sarah," he said. "I'm beginning to suspect there's something going on between her and James—the plumber. I'm not very good at figuring these things out, so I may be completely off base."

"What are the signs?"

"Well, she spent the entire day helping us in the basement. And she hates the basement. I have to pay her to go down there to flip a circuit breaker."

"And?"

"And she was laughing at all his stories. Believe me, they were not that funny. He was telling plumbing stories. Plumbing isn't funny. Backed-up pipes... flooded bathrooms. Not funny."

"Yup, sounds like she's got a crush on him," Amelia said, nodding. "Did she touch him?"

He gasped. "In front of me?"

"Not... I'm not talking about a...you know...a—"

"A hand job?"

"Yes, a hand job, to be precise. I'm talking about a casual touch. Did she put her hand on his arm when she was laughing or did she brush a piece of lint off his shirt?"

"Yes!" he cried. "Yes to both. And then she kept touching his tools. Not his—you know—his pipe wrench."

Amelia laughed. "I got that. His wrench. I would agree that there's something going on there. Maybe she's falling in love."

"With a plumber," he murmured.

"It wouldn't be the worst choice in the world for an innkeeper. Not like an art historian," Amelia teased.

He gave her an odd look and Amelia instantly regretted what she'd said. They could certainly talk about a romance between Sarah and James, but it was way too early to examine their own relationship too closely. Sure, she was just making a joke, but maybe he didn't find her jokes funny, either.

"I think we're great together," he said.

"Do you?" she asked. "I mean, I do, too."

He pulled her into his arms and kissed her, lingering over her mouth as he teased her with his tongue. Every time he kissed her, Amelia wondered if it would ever seem ordinary or unremarkable. But then he would do something that would make her knees feel like jelly and they were off again, down a whole new road to sexual satisfaction.

He pulled back and looked down at her. "What are you thinking about?"

"Right now?"

He nodded.

"I was thinking that your kisses were like James's plumbing stories. I'm the only one in the world who can truly appreciate them."

He chuckled. "You're the strangest woman I've ever known."

"I'm glad you believe that," Amelia said. "Your expectations won't be quite so high."

"Maybe you're perfect for me," he said.

She didn't answer. Instead Amelia wrapped her arms around his neck and kissed him. She pulled him toward the bed, her fingers working at the buttons of his shirt. By the time she pushed him down on the mattress, his shirt was on the floor. Next, she worked on his damp boots, tugging them off along with his socks. With single-minded efficiency, she removed every last item of clothing from his body until there was nothing left to do but stare at him.

He grinned. "Now, what are you going to do with me?"

Amelia returned his smile. "I'll look at you every now and then. But I should probably finish my work." She sat on the floor and picked up her papers, rearranging them and then fastening them onto a clipboard.

"And I'm just supposed to lie here?"

Amelia nodded, then glanced over her shoulder. "You could come down here and help me. You could be my manservant. My naked manservant."

He moved to sit next to her and she pointed to a spot across from her. "Right there. So I can enjoy the view."

Grudgingly, he sat on the rug, crossing his legs in front of him. "This is strange. You are a very peculiar woman. Why don't you take your clothes off, too?"

"Because this is my fantasy, not yours," Amelia said. She handed him the clipboard. "I want you to read the description line. So I can make sure I got all of these."

"Your fantasy involves old silver? That's really weird, Amelia." He held up his hand. "Just being honest. Also, it's not all that warm in here."

"Actually, my fantasy has to do with a deserted tropical island. We're living there and we don't have to wear clothes because we're all alone on the island."

"Then why aren't you naked?"

"Because it's not that warm in here and I wanted to finish my work." She glanced up at him. "Not so weird anymore, is it? Oh, and then there's my manservant fantasy. In that one I have a very handsome man who caters to my every whim. And he does that while naked." She released a slow breath. "And erect."

"I'd assume you're not referring to my posture," Sam murmured.

"No," she said with a coy smile, her gaze dropping to his lap.

He crawled across the space between them and dropped a kiss on her lips. "If you want to speed that fantasy along, you'd take your clothes off, crawl under the covers with me and try to warm me up."

She reached down and wrapped her fingers around his growing erection. "You feel warm enough to me," she murmured.

"Are you taking advantage of your manservant? There are many other things I can provide you with, madam. You only need to ask."

He stood, pulled her to her feet and began to strip the clothes off her body. When she was naked, Amelia ran to the bed and yanked the covers up, inadvertently sending her papers and books flying. She let out a little scream when he caught her around the waist and pulled her down onto the bed.

"Don't you want to know how much your silver collection is worth?" she asked, wriggling beneath him.

"How much?" Sam murmured, his lips already finding the ticklish spot on her neck.

"Without the potential Revere, about seventy-six thousand. Give or take five thousand."

He pushed up, bracing his hands on either side of her head. "Are you kidding me?"

Amelia shook her head, pleased to see his reaction. "That's a conservative estimate. Some of it could go for more at auction. And I'm still waiting for appraisals from my friend on a couple of odd pieces that didn't have a hallmark. If you have another Revere, it could be even more."

He was silent for a long time before slowly shaking his head. "Kind of ironic. I have the riches of silver, yet I'm cash poor."

"Why can't you sell it?" she asked.

"It belongs to the family. To the inn. My grandfather sold this bed for cash and look where it got us. What if I make the same mistake?"

"But couldn't you use the silver as collateral?" she asked.

"It's a risk," he said. "And it didn't work with the Revere mug. When I mentioned it, George at the bank patted me on the back and treated me like I was his crazy old uncle trying to pawn trash as treasure."

"I'm sorry," she said. "I wish I could help."

Sam rolled her over on top of him. "It's okay, I convinced him to give me the loan anyway. Besides, this helps," he murmured. "Believe me."

As he pulled her into a passionate kiss, she realized she'd been right. He was too proud to accept anyone's help, even when he had nowhere else to turn.
And though he needed her body, and all the passions
and pleasures that came with it, he wouldn't accept
anything else. She ought to be happy. It was perfect
for two people who wanted nothing more than a good
time in bed. No strings. No hard feelings when she
walked away.

So why did the realization make her so sad?

IT HADN'T TAKEN much convincing to lure Amelia out of
the display window and over to the inn the next afternoon. The ever-deepening snow had worried Sam and
he didn't want to have her stuck all alone while he dealt
with things at the inn.

Even though they were in the midst of a road-closing
blizzard, the wedding party, scheduled to arrive that
evening, had decided they were coming anyway. They'd
take the early train north and expected Sam to transport
them from the station in Millhaven to the inn. Though
they'd originally planned to have the ceremony at the
Presbyterian church in nearby Hudson, the minister had
agreed to marry them at the inn. Sarah was in charge
of transforming the dining room into a proper venue
for the ceremony.

"Thank God you're here, Amelia," Sarah said as
they walked in the front door. "I could use a pair of
hands helping me with all this fussy décor. Sam is no
help at all."

"You need my help?"

"Isn't that why you came?" Sarah asked.

"She's a guest," Sam said. "You can't put her to work."

"Of course you can," Amelia said, glancing over at Sam and giving him a smile. "What is it we're doing?"

"Decorating for a wedding," Sarah said.

"Who is getting married?" Amelia asked.

"We have thirty-some guests arriving later today. We've decided to have the ceremony here because of the snow. It's a small group. But I want to make it nice."

"I can help you with that," Amelia said.

Sam sat back and marveled as the two of them formulated their plans. He was ordered to fetch specific objects from the rooms and the attic and the kitchen and he quietly did what he was told.

He was walking through the front parlor when he noticed someone outside shoveling the front walk. He shouted a greeting and was surprised to find out it was James beneath the heavy, hooded coat. He motioned for the plumber to come inside and James nodded, leaving the shovel in the snowbank beside the walk.

"What are you doing?"

"Oh, Sarah said she had a lot of work to do getting ready for the wedding this weekend, so I thought I'd give her a hand. I brought my tools along. I was going to go 'round and replace the washers on all the faucets."

"You were just going to do that for no reason?" Sam asked.

"I was going to do it for Sarah," he said sheepishly.

"What's going on with you two?"

Sam noticed a flush rise in James's already-pink

cheeks. "I'm not sure. I kind of think she might like me. I like her a lot. Ever since high school, I thought she was the prettiest girl in Millhaven. And when she went away to college, I was hoping she'd come back here someday and I'd get the chance to tell her."

"She graduated from college four years ago," Sam said. "What's taken you so long?"

"I guess I was waiting for my big moment. I figure a guy's got only one, maybe two, chances to convince a woman that he loves her. And if he doesn't get it done, she'll just move along and find someone else she wants. I'm not sure Sarah was ready to hear it from me last year or the year before. But yesterday, when I was here working on your boiler, I kinda felt that she was ready."

"Well, I have to say you may be right on that one."

"Really? Did she say something to you?"

"No. But I've never seen her act like such an idiot around a man. Except for that time she met some guy from a boy band."

"The Backstreet Boys," he said. "She really loved them. Had pictures up on her locker at school."

"Well, why don't you grab a cup of coffee and warm up? We can finish this up later. It doesn't pay to shovel if it's still snowing."

Sam followed the other man into the dining room and watched his sister's reaction when she spotted the plumber.

It was all there in her smile, in the sparkle in her eyes. He looked over at Amelia and saw her smiling at the pair. "Sarah, James said he'd fix our drippy faucets.

Why don't you show him the fixtures that need new washers? Amelia and I will work on the dining room."

"How are you with flowers?" Sarah asked.

"Me?" Amelia said. "Oh, I'm very good with flowers. It was one of those things that my mother thought was important for a young lady to learn."

"Great. The boxes are in the big fridge. Why don't you make the arrangements? Once I have room in the fridge, I can make the wedding cake. I can get that done tonight."

"What should I use for vases?"

"There are lots of vases on the shelves in the mud-room. I'd mix the pewter with crystal."

"You have pewter?" Amelia asked. She shook her head. "You realize that Revere worked in pewter, too?"

"We can have you appraise that later," Sam said.

"How'd that go, by the way?" Sarah asked.

"We'll talk about it after the weekend," Sam said.

"Why don't you get the silver out of my truck and we can use some of the less valuable pieces for the wedding?"

"There are more valuable pieces?" Sarah asked.

Sam nodded. "I'll show you later. You and I are going to have to make some decisions."

Sarah and James wandered off to find leaky faucets and Sam and Amelia sat at the dining room table to work on the flowers.

"He's in love with her," Sam said.

"And she's in love with him," Amelia added.

"Really?"

Amelia nodded. "The minute you left the room, she found a way to bring him up."

Sam thought about the match for a moment. "I guess it wouldn't be a bad thing. We'd have a plumber in the family. If I could just find a lady electrician to marry, we'd be set."

Amelia grabbed a wilted flower and tossed it at him. "You're supposed to marry for love, not union membership." She paused. "Have you ever thought about getting married?"

Sam shrugged. "I haven't spent much time on it. I'm pretty much married to this job. I'd have to find someone willing to devote the rest of their life to this place. Not such an appealing choice."

"That's not true," Amelia said.

"Well, let's just say I haven't had women beating down the door to get at me."

"I think you're so used to looking at this place in a negative way that you can no longer see all the wonderful things about it. You're living in a lovely, historical home and you're sharing your home with people who appreciate it. You live in a town where everyone knows you. It's safe and quiet here. You're surrounded by nature."

"And yet I can't feel grateful," Sam said, a cynical edge to his voice.

"It isn't always going to be like this," she said as she began to arrange a small vase of flowers. "Life does change. Maybe Sarah and James will get married and they'll take care of the inn, giving you a chance to do something new. Or maybe you'll meet a woman who always dreamed of running an inn. Maybe all four of you will run the inn. There are a lot of different ways your life could change. But you have to let it."

She took a deep breath and pushed her first arrangement in front of him. "This is going to be such a nice wedding. When I was going to marry Edward, I wanted to have a very small, intimate wedding like this. I wanted to do it in an art museum. Of course, my mother wouldn't have it. She had at least three hundred people on her list alone. And Edward's mother was just as bad. Imagine attending your own wedding with six hundred people you'd never even met."

"So you were happy not to go through with it?" Sam asked.

"Yes, it wasn't what I wanted," Amelia replied.

"And how does he feel?"

"He hopes I'll come to my senses, but that's only because he doesn't want to spend the time finding an alternative. It would take searching and dating and actually trying to be romantic. Edward just doesn't have the patience for all that nonsense."

"That's the best part, though," Sam said.

She smiled. "I know. I'm just beginning to realize that." Amelia slowly turned the vase, examining the arrangement from all sides. "So, what do you think? Will it do?"

"Definitely," he said. "You're a woman of many talents."

"Now you have to make one just like this," she said.

They spent the next hour finishing the arrangements. It was a chance to talk, without any thought of seduction invading the conversation. Sam realized that if they were in a real relationship, this would be an ordinary day for them, enjoying conversation, working on a task together, laughing and joking.

"What would you think about spending the night here?" Sam asked. "No one is going to come to watch us at Benny's in the middle of this snowstorm. And I'd rather we were here, warm and comfortable, than sleeping in that drafty window."

"That would be nice. We could have dinner with Sarah and James. And we could make a fire. And have pie."

"We can have pie right now," he said. He pulled her to her feet and followed her into the kitchen. But before she opened the pie safe, Sam wrapped his arms around her waist and lifted her up on the edge of the counter. Cupping her face in his hands, Sam kissed her, taking in the delicious taste of her mouth.

His hands skimmed over her body, then slipped beneath her sweater. Sam knew every inch of her body. So when his palm cupped her breast, he knew exactly how perfectly the soft flesh would fit in his hand and how, with just a gentle coax, her nipple would harden into a peak.

If they had a future, would their days together be punctuated with moments such as these, when they'd forget the ordinary tasks and drift into a haze of passion? "Pretty soon we're going to have to decide what to do about that damned bed," he murmured.

"What bed?" she asked.

He pulled back, and when their gazes met, Amelia

smiled. "I'm just kidding. But it doesn't seem quite so important when you're kissing me. Besides, I know you're going to give it to me."

"Yeah?"

She nodded. "I think you realize how important it is for me. The only reason you haven't given in yet is because you enjoy having me around. And if I agreed to give the bed back to you after the exhibit, I believe you might cave."

"I believe that's a compromise, isn't it?" Sam asked.

"A good one, in fact. I might be able to convince Vivian to consider the bed a loan."

"I'll consider your offer and get back to you."

"What if I demand a decision now or I'll put on my shoes and go home?" she asked.

Sam nodded. "I figure you have other reasons to stay. Pie. Your whole manservant fantasy. My pewter collection. Your flower-arranging talents."

"And there's the sex," Amelia said. "Don't forget the sex."

"There is that. So," Sam said, "pie or sex?"

"Pie with sex?" Amelia countered.

"I'll meet you in the George Washington room. Get the key from behind the desk. Room number twelve."

With a laugh, Amelia jumped off the counter and headed through the dining room. Sam grabbed a half-eaten apple pie from the pie safe, then stopped for a can of whipped cream before following after Amelia, trying not to give in to the feeling that this fantasy they were living was fast coming to an end. And he had no idea how to keep it going.

SAM AND AMELIA settled into the old stone kitchen for the weekend. Amelia was glad to be out of the display window and warm and cozy at the inn. Sam kept a crackling fire going in the hearth.

They worked together, getting the inn ready for the wedding, and every now and then they'd escape to their little stone cottage to enjoy each other in more carnal ways. But Amelia sensed the end coming, waiting just beyond the edge of their reality.

She wasn't sure how it would happen, what they'd say or what promises they'd try to make. Maybe it would be a simple goodbye, a quick kiss and a vague promise to see each other when she returned the bed. Life would go on. She could live without Sam Blackstone, as hard as that was to believe right now.

Amelia told herself to live in the present. And in the present, they were naked again, caught up in their passion. Amelia smiled down at him, her legs straddling his hips, his shaft buried deep inside her.

"Don't move," he murmured.

"Don't tell me what to do," she teased.

"All right, move."

"I said, don't tell me what to do."

Sam chuckled softly, reaching up to caress her breast. "What are you thinking?"

"I'm trying to figure out if there's a third choice. Move, don't move or…"

"There aren't any gray areas here, Millie."

She smiled, then tightened the muscles where they were joined. She'd always wondered if that was something a man could feel but she'd never had the courage to try or ask. She watched a smile curl the corners of his mouth.

"What are you doing to me?" he murmured.

"I'm not moving," she said.

He closed his eyes, losing himself in the sensations she was creating for him. Amelia smiled as she watched desire suffuse his expression and then as it started to affect the rest of his body.

He grasped her waist, his fingers holding her firmly against him. They'd made love in so many different ways, and along the way, she'd learned to read his responses, to know when he was close. There were certain things that drove him over the edge quickly and others that he could enjoy for a long, lazy afternoon.

Sam was so adventurous when it came to sex that Amelia found herself caught up in his pleasure. She wasn't embarrassed to express her own needs, something she would never have done in the past. Sex was pleasure and passion and perfection, and it was something that belonged to the two of them.

Amelia started to move at a quick pace and Sam growled softly, his fingers digging into her hips. A moment later he arched against her, his body tense and aching for release. He seemed to linger there, at the very edge, for longer than he ever had before.

And then the powerful shudder shook his body and the orgasm took hold. He drove into her, even deeper than before, and Amelia enjoyed the power she held over his body.

They'd exchanged the battle for the bed into a battle for sexual satisfaction. Control ebbed and flowed between them, each generous in the give and greedy in the take.

There were endless possibilities in their passion and Amelia wondered if there was enough time to explore them all before she got too old for sex. She stared down at him, and when Sam opened his eyes, she smiled.

"We should take a little break before you kill me," he said.

She crawled off him, fetched a box she'd left on the table and brought it back to the bed. "You could help me with these," she said. She dumped the box on the bed and he picked up a bag of candy-coated almonds and tore it open.

Amelia took the bag from him. "You can't eat those. They're for the table favors."

"What are table favors?" Sam asked.

"For the wedding," she explained. "They're just little treats that you spread around the tables. People can munch on them or take them home. Here, I'll show you."

She cut out a square of tulle and dumped a handful of the pastel-colored almonds in the center. Pulling up the corners, she made a little bag and tied the top with a lavender ribbon. "The bride's colors are pale lavender and ice blue."

"Her colors?"

Amelia giggled. "You don't know anything about planning a wedding, do you?"

"Am I supposed to? When do they teach you about stuff like this? I've never seen purple almonds before. Where do you get these?"

"They're traditional," she said. "Weddings are filled with tradition."

"And this is all written down somewhere in some official book?"

She handed him scissors and a piece of tulle. "Lots of books. Just follow that piece as a pattern."

Sam sat up and crossed his legs in front him. He spread the quilt over his lap and turned his attention to the wispy netting. "You like this stuff, don't you?"

"Every girl dreams about her wedding," she murmured. "When my mother hired a wedding planner, I was crushed. I wanted to do the whole thing myself."

"Why didn't you?"

"The guest list was over six hundred people, remember. And with the budget that comes along with so many people, Mother wanted to turn it over to a professional. It was for the best, though."

"Why is that?"

"Maybe, if I had planned it myself, I would have been more willing to go through with it. And getting married would have been a mistake."

"Just with that guy, though, right?"

Amelia thought about his question for a long moment and shrugged. "I don't know. I've spent so much of my life trying to please someone else while they tried to control every aspect of my life. My parents. And then Edward to a lesser extent. I don't want to live my life worried that I'm not living up to someone else's standards."

"That sounds like a pretty strong argument against happily-ever-after," he said.

"Who says you can't live happily ever after without being married?" Sam handed her a square of tulle and she smiled. "Good. That's nice. What about you? Do you ever think about getting married?"

"I think about *being* married," Sam said. "Not so much about *getting* married."

"That's the way to do it," she said. "The wedding is just a big party. The marriage is for the rest of your life."

"And that's the problem," he said with a soft chuckle. "Who'd want to be a part of my nightmare?"

"Is it really that bad?"

"I've had three semi-serious relationships since I took over the inn. And they were all with women who thought running an inn was the most romantic profession in the world. Until they realized that you actually have to run an inn when you're an innkeeper. It doesn't run itself. They all opted out shortly after finding out it wasn't all that romantic."

She shook her head, smiling. "Aren't we a sad pair. No almonds for us." She held up a completed favor and then dropped it into a small box. "I sound so cynical."

"I don't know. Maybe we're being realistic," Sam said.

She leaned over and dropped a kiss onto his lips. "After this, will you help me polish silverware?"

"You're a guest here. How is it you've been assigned chores?"

Amelia shrugged. "I can't leave with this snow, and Sarah needs help, so I offered to give her a hand with the chores. This is an important weekend for the inn."

Sam slowly shook his head. "I can't understand how any man would ever let you go."

The words hung between them for a long time and Amelia wasn't sure she wanted to explain all that had happened between her and Edward. There were still times when she questioned her decision to leave him. He was a good man and he'd wanted nothing but the best for her.

"He didn't let me go," she said. "I walked away."

"No regrets?"

"Of course I have regrets," Amelia said. "I hurt him. I regret that. I think he really does love me, in his own way. I'm just not sure that he isn't settling. Someday he'll meet a woman who'll knock him off his feet and he'll understand passion and desire."

"He still loves you?"

Amelia wanted to change the subject, but she knew once Sam asked a question, he usually required an answer. "I believe so."

"How can you be sure?"

She carefully tied a ribbon on another bag of almonds. "We…we haven't really broken up. Not officially. Not technically. We're just…taking a break."

Sam stared at her for a long moment. "I don't get it. Either you're together or you aren't. You can't—"

"We aren't," Amelia insisted.

"You say you aren't. What would Edward say?"

She avoided his gaze, turning back to the almonds spread on the quilt in front of her. She began to sort them by color. "I have no idea what he'd say. I just didn't want to hurt him. He's a good guy and he's just trying to please his family. I told him I needed time. He said he'd wait till I was ready to come back."

"How long has it been?"

"Almost a year."

"That's a mighty big torch to be carrying," he said.

Sam dropped back on the bed, throwing his arm over his eyes. "What are we doing here, Millie? And don't say we're making wedding favors." He looked over at her. "Is this just going to end when you go home to Boston?"

"I think it has to."

"Because you're still engaged to Edward."

"We're not engaged," Amelia said. "There's just this tiny string that we haven't snipped yet. A single string, nothing more."

"All right, you're not engaged," Sam corrected. "He still is."

"That doesn't change anything between us. It doesn't make me feel any differently about you than I did before. And it has nothing to do with our situation. This has to end because I need my own life."

Sam crawled out of bed and began to gather his clothes from the floor. Amelia didn't know what to say to him. They hadn't made any commitments to each other. And she was sure that he was having as hard of a time as she was trying to picture how they could make a relationship work.

There was no doubt that she cared about him. And it wasn't impossible to believe she might be in love with him. But they'd known each other for less than a week. How could someone possibly be sure of their true feelings in such a short time?

"I should check in with Sarah and see what's going on."

Amelia rolled off the bed and crossed the room to where he stood. She wrapped her arms around his waist and hugged her body to his. He was so warm, so strong. She didn't want to think about what her life would be like without him. But Amelia knew better than anyone that romantic relationships had to conform to the realities of everyday life. She'd tried to picture a life here in Millhaven or a life with Sam in Boston and she'd failed.

Love wasn't simple. Even in the best of circumstances—with time and money and family support—it didn't always work out. Add in their issues and it was impossible. She took his hand and led him to the bed, pulling him down beside her.

"I can't say what's going to happen with us," she said. "I don't think you can, either. We can only wait and see. Hopefully we won't put pressure on each other to make it something it truly isn't."

"I need to know it isn't going to end when you drive away. Promise me."

She pushed up on her toes and kissed his lips. "I promise. I have to bring the bed back, remember. We'll talk again then."

He covered her mouth with his, pulling her into a deep kiss. This was no longer a simple affair. Feelings had changed, strings had been attached and Sam was no longer existing in the present. He'd been thinking about the future.

Everything had changed. From this moment on, Amelia wasn't just a friend with benefits. She was Sam Blackstone's lover. He was in her life now and he wasn't sure he wanted to leave. But Amelia wasn't convinced he really wanted her to stay, either.

7

THE VALENTINE'S DAY nor'easter was turning into one for the record books. The snow had been falling continuously for more than forty-eight hours, blowing into drifts that had closed roads and made travel nearly impossible.

The trains were still running, though no one was sure when that might change. For now, the wedding party was due to arrive at 6:33 p.m. on the Empire Builder out of Penn Station. James had agreed to help ferry the guests from the station to the inn, and Sarah and Amelia were working on a late buffet supper for the group to enjoy upon their arrival.

Sam had grabbed James to help with splitting additional wood that would be needed for the fireplaces in each room. They'd bundled up and headed for the woodpile stacked against the rear wall of the stone kitchen.

They'd worked out a nice rhythm, with James balancing logs on the block and Sam splitting them into three pieces. They didn't speak, just worked, and Sam was grateful for the silence. He had enough on his mind to make idle conversation.

"Do you want me to split the wood for a while?" James shouted over the blustery wind.

"Do you want to?" Sam asked.

"I could use the exercise."

Sam nodded and handed the ax to James, then took his spot next to the block. To his surprise, James handled the ax as well as he did. He'd always considered the plumber a bit of a goof, but the more he got to know him, the more he liked about the other man. He was quiet and humble, clever and witty, and he knew a helluva lot more about fixing stuff than Sam ever would.

"That's enough," Sam shouted after another ten minutes of chopping. Each room had already been stocked with enough wood for the night. They'd leave the extra in canvas slings on the back porch, ready to be delivered to the rooms when needed.

As they worked at this task, James began to chat about the weather. But the more he rattled on about low pressure systems and upper atmosphere moisture, the more Sam wanted to ask him about Sarah. There was no decent segue into the conversation, so Sam just blurted out his question. "What are your intentions with my sister?"

James didn't seem surprised by the question and he grinned. "I fully intend to marry that girl. I planned to ask your father if that was all right, but since he isn't around, I suppose I should ask you."

"Don't you think this is a little quick?"

"I've known her since I was a freshman in high school. That's when I fell in love with her for the first time. So, as far as I'm concerned, we've known each other long enough."

"You seem so sure," Sam said.

"No doubts."

"But how can you be so certain?"

"I try to imagine my life without her," James said. "And I don't like the way it looks."

"You've got a good job," Sam said.

"I enjoy working around the inn, too. I can help you with a lot of the jobs here. Sarah wants to raise a family in Millhaven."

Sam had never really talked about the future with his sister. He was thankful for every day she stuck around to help him, assuming she stayed only out of duty and guilt. But apparently she was happy with her life in Millhaven.

"Hell, this inn is a great place to raise a family."

Sam shook his head. Sarah had never even mentioned her dreams of having a family. In truth, he'd assumed she hated working at the inn as much as he did.

James pushed to his feet and brushed the snow off the back of his jeans. "Can I ask you something?"

"Sure."

"I'm trying to decide about a ring. It's Valentine's Day tomorrow and I can't decide whether I should give her the ring I bought or if I should take her to pick one out."

"Wait! When did you buy a ring for her?"

"Four years ago. When she came back to Millhaven after college."

"I gotta give you credit. You know what you want. But I think it might be a little too early to ask her. You've only just started…" Sam paused. "Have you even had a date?"

James frowned. "Not exactly. You're saying I should ask her on a date first."

"Yeah, I mean, that's usually the way it goes."

James thought about that for a long moment, then shook his head. "Nah, I'm just going to get right to it. I'm going to propose. There's always time to date after she says yes."

"What if she doesn't say yes?"

He shrugged. "I'll just keep asking until she does. I'm sure she's the one. I'm not going to let her get away."

Sam couldn't help but admire the guy's resolve. He knew what he wanted and he was willing to risk everything to get it. And unlike most men, James was also ready to accept failure and had already come up with a contingency plan.

As they stacked the wood on the porch, Sam began to think about his options with Amelia. He'd always assumed that a marriage proposal to any woman would come after a long and steady relationship and careful consideration of her enthusiasm for inn-keeping.

He'd never considered making a proposal partially for shock value. But at least with a proposal, she'd be forced to weigh him and Edward equally. Then again, she might also just laugh in his face, and unlike James,

Sam wasn't sure his ego would survive that kind of response.

"Why don't you go back inside and give Sarah a hand?" Sam said. "I'll finish up here."

"You sure?"

"Yeah. Tell Amelia I'll be in soon."

As he continued to stack firewood, Sam considered his next move. When he and Amelia were in bed together, it seemed as if everything was perfect. She needed him and wanted him. He was the only person who could satisfy her. But sex wasn't everything. Hell, until recently, she was ready to marry a man who was mediocre in the bedroom.

It was obvious that she considered other things more important than passion. Things such as independence. And she'd admitted that she hadn't completely broken things off with Edward. Did that mean she hadn't quite rejected her parents' values, either? That she still wanted someone with financial security and family connections? Who had social standing and an Ivy League education? Unfortunately he fell short in a few of those areas. Hell, he fell short in all of them.

So, he was good in bed. He had that going on, but that was about it. And he could split wood. He doubted that Edward could manage that with his soft, little city-boy hands.

"What are you doing out here!"

Sam turned to find Amelia standing on the back porch, bundled in one of Sarah's down jackets and a pair of fleece-lined boots. A scarf covered most of her face. He'd never seen anything quite so cute.

"Stacking firewood," he said. "I suspect there are going to be plenty of fires laid this weekend. Fires are so romantic."

She came up to him and wrapped her arms around his waist. "Yes, they are. And there's a lovely one burning in the front parlor right now. Why don't you come and enjoy it with me for a bit before you have to go pick up your guests?"

"I have to finish this," he said.

"Then I'll help you," she said. She followed him to the stone kitchen and began to gather wood, tucking the logs beneath her arms.

"You don't have to do that," he said.

"I want to help you," she said.

"Go back inside, Amelia. I can finish this on my own." She refused to listen to him, and as he watched her stumble through the snow, Sam felt his anger build. She'd grown up in the lap of luxury. She'd probably had servants to wait on her hand and foot. There was a standard of living that she was accustomed to and it was a far cry from what he could ever offer her.

As she walked to the stone kitchen, Sam grabbed her. She shrieked and dropped the wood. He picked her up off her feet, tossed her over his shoulder and carried her to the porch. "Go inside."

Stubbornly she shook her head. The moment he turned, Amelia raced past him toward the pile of logs. But the snow was too deep and she tripped and fell face-first into the soft powder. Sam hurried to her side and she rolled over, her face covered with snow and the sound of her laughter drifting on the wind.

"I tripped," she said, wiping the snow out of her eyes.

"You could have hurt yourself," he said. "Broken a bone or knocked your teeth out."

She grabbed a handful of snow and threw it at his face. "Oh, lighten up. It's snow. It's supposed to be fun."

He tried to grab her arm to pull her to her feet, but she threw another handful of snow at him. Sam threw his leg over her waist, pinning her to the ground, then grabbed her wrists and held them on either side of her head.

"I'm not going to kiss you," she said, giggling.

"And I'm not going to kiss you," he said.

She wriggled beneath him, trying to escape. But she was laughing so hard, she could barely catch her breath. She was so beautiful his heart ached when he looked at her. He'd never wanted a woman more than he wanted her. But he had no idea how to keep her.

"Why are you still here?" he asked.

"Because you're sitting on top of me," she said, slapping him on the chest.

"No. I mean why are you still here in Millhaven? We came to a compromise on the bed. So why haven't you gone home to Boston?"

Her expression shifted as she heard the frustration in his voice. She stared at him for a long moment, her gaze fixed to his, and this time, when she tried to get up, Sam rolled to the side to allow it.

Amelia got to her feet. "I—I thought you wanted me to stay a little longer. And you said you were considering our compromise on the bed. You never told me that you'd made the final decision."

"And what if I had? What if I'd said, 'Go ahead. Take the bed.' Would you have left?"

She tugged at the scarf around her neck, then with a soft curse ripped it off and threw it into the snow. "You're talking in circles. Why are you angry with me?"

"I'm not angry," Sam said, heading toward the inn.

She followed him as he strode through the snow.

When he reached the porch, he stopped. "Go inside. We'll talk about this later."

He felt her hand on his shoulder and he slowly turned to face her. Tiny drops of melted snow clung to her lashes and her cheeks were pink from the cold. Sam fought the impulse to drag her into his arms and kiss her.

"Why won't you let me help you? I don't understand you at all," she said, shaking her head.

"Welcome to the club," he muttered. "'Cause I'm not sure who the hell I am right now, either."

"You're a stubborn man who would rather be a martyr than be happy."

With that, Amelia turned and walked inside, slamming the door behind her.

THE REMAINDER OF the day was a mad rush of activity. The guests arrived just after 7:00 p.m. and Amelia helped Sarah with check-in while Sam showed the guests to their rooms and James brought them their luggage.

There was barely a moment to think about the confrontation she and Sam had in the backyard. Amelia wasn't even sure what it was all about. First he wanted her to stay and now he was wondering why she hadn't left. He'd never fully agreed to give her the bed, but suddenly he had. He felt threatened by Edward but couldn't see that her reservations had nothing to do with Sam's pedigree.

The bride and groom arrived in a whirlwind of snow and excitement. They were both profusely grateful for Sam's flexibility in making their wedding work in the middle of a nor'easter. Sarah and Amelia explained the details, menus, wedding décor and a finalized schedule, while the bridal couple nodded their agreement.

Every now and then, Amelia caught Sam's gaze from across the room. His emotions were much harder to read. They served a buffet dinner in the dining room and the group had scattered themselves between the common rooms, talking and laughing. When the bride and groom retired to their separate rooms, the rest of the party gradually made their way to their own rooms, leaving a peaceful silence behind them.

Amelia stood at the kitchen sink, rinsing dessert plates as Sarah loaded them in the dishwasher. "I think that went very well," Sarah said.

"I think so, too," Amelia agreed.

"Thank you for all your help. I'm not sure what I would have done without you."

"I didn't do that much," Amelia replied.

"Yes, you did. And it was more fun working with someone. I had a really good time."

"It was nice that your friend stuck around to help." Amelia frowned. "Where is James?"

"I sent him to bed." Sarah smiled. "My bed." She wiped her hands on a kitchen towel, then jumped up to sit on the edge of the counter. "The more he hangs around, the more I realize how...adorable he is. Why has it taken me so long to notice?"

"Maybe there's a right moment for everyone. A moment when two people are completely open to falling in love. Like a tiny window of time where all the stars align perfectly and all the wishes you've had for your life come true. Maybe you and James are just...there."

Sarah nodded. "I never even considered him and now he's all I can think about. He's sweet and kind and funny. And he says I'm beautiful and interesting and smart. I'm falling in love with him."

"Really?"

Sarah nodded. "And I can't seem to stop smiling."

"I'm going to finish up here. Why don't you go find your James and tell him exactly what you told me?"

"Yeah? You think I should tell him?"

Amelia nodded. "Always trust your heart." It had been the only thing that had gotten her through her breakup with Edward. Deep in her heart, she'd known marrying him would be wrong. And she'd tried to convince him of that. But he'd refused to accept the truth, certain that she'd realize her mistake and come back to him.

Sarah hopped down from the counter and gave Amelia a quick hug. "Thanks," she murmured.

"No problem."

She watched Sarah hurry out of the kitchen before turning back to the last few dishes in the sink. Maybe she hadn't completely ended things with Edward to give herself a safety net. As insurance in case everything else in her life fell apart, she'd have at least one person who'd still love her.

She'd thought herself so brave to walk away from her family and make a new life for herself. But in truth, there were a few strings she hadn't snipped.

Was she in love with Sam? It felt as if he'd invaded her heart and her soul, and she could no longer tell where she ended and he began. He could pull her into his arms and they'd fit, perfectly, as if they'd been made especially for each other.

And yet there was something holding her back, keeping her from admitting exactly what it was that frightened her about him. She'd always suspected that honesty was the most important quality in a relationship. She had to do exactly as she'd urged Sarah to do: trust her heart and tell him how she felt.

She put the last dish in the drainer and wiped her hands on a towel.

"What are you doing, Amelia?"

She spun around to find Sam standing in the kitchen doorway, his shoulder braced against the doorjamb. "Just finishing up for Sarah."

The tension that had followed them around since their encounter in the snow was still there, invisible yet palpable. He didn't seem angry, Amelia mused. Just… Her gaze scanned his features, searching for a clue.

She cleared her throat. "I was thinking, if the roads are clear, I'll leave on Monday. I'm a little worried about hauling that trailer if there's ice."

He shook his head. "You don't have to leave. I don't want you to leave."

A wave of tears rushed over her and she tried to fight them back. What was this game he was playing with her? She didn't understand the rules. "What do you want?" she asked, a single tear slipping from the corner of her eye. "Why are you doing this to me?"

"Look at yourself," he said. "Are you happy doing this? Washing dishes? Making beds? Stacking firewood?"

"I was trying to help you," she said. "You could say 'thank you' like your sister did instead of acting as if I've done something wrong."

"Thank you," he murmured.

"You're welcome." She threw the towel down and tried to get past him at the door. But he caught her arm and pulled her in front of him.

"Don't try to convince yourself that this life is for you, Millie." He leaned close, his breath warm on her cheek. "Don't tell yourself that you can be happy here, because you can't. It may seem like a pleasant way to pass a few days, but, believe me, it will suck the happiness out of you over time."

"Do you really hate it all that much?" she asked.

"I hate that I can't offer you more than this," he muttered.

"Is that what this is all about?" Amelia asked. "Are you still comparing yourself to Edward?"

"Edward. Your family. Your friends. It's a whole different existence, Millie. You come from a world where people wait on you. You don't wait on people."

"You really don't know me at all, do you? I lived that life and I never felt as if it fit. I tried to turn myself into one of them, but I couldn't. For them—my parents, Edward, his parents—money is everything. It's happiness and success. But I always thought that love made a person happy and successful." She inhaled a ragged breath. "I told you before, money can't buy happiness."

"I've never believed that. Money buys boilers and new roofs and water heaters and copper plumbing. Money buys a decent sleep at night and worry-free days. It buys time away from a job that feels as if it's going to smother you alive."

"If money is so important to you, then you could always marry me," Amelia said.

He frowned. "What did you say?"

"You heard me. You could marry me. Remember? I inherit ten million dollars when I get married. Ten million would buy a lot of water heaters."

"I'm not going to marry you for your money," he said.

"And why not? Don't you believe that money buys happiness? It seems like you'd jump at that kind of chance."

"I just won't do it."

"Because you don't want to be happy. You could leave the inn if you wanted to. Your father would understand if you wanted to sell it. Sarah and James would probably take it from you. But you'd rather suffer. And that's why I can't stay. Because if I did, I'd twist myself into knots to make you happy. Just like

I did with my parents." She reached out and took his hand. "And then we'd both be miserable."

"Is this the end, then? Because I don't want it to be," Sam said.

She grasped his other hand. "I don't know what to do with these feelings any more than you do," Amelia assured him, her voice soft and pleading. "It doesn't have to be goodbye. Maybe in time we'll get it sorted out. Find a way we can both be happy."

"So how do we do that?" he asked, pulling her wrist to his lips. He pressed a kiss to her pulse point, then wrapped her arm around his neck.

"We live three hours apart," she said. "It's not like you're on a different planet. I could spend every weekend here. You could spend every weekend in Boston."

"I have an inn to run," he reminded her.

"You have Sarah," she said. "And James."

Sam smiled. "That does look hopeful."

"Our plans don't have to be carved in stone."

"No, they don't."

She pressed a soft kiss to his lips, her palm smoothing over his cheek. "Can we go to bed now? We have an early day tomorrow and I could really use some sleep. I'm tired of fighting with you."

"We don't usually sleep when we go to bed," he said.

"I realize that. But tonight we need to be practical and try to ignore our desires for just one night. Do you think you can manage that?"

"I can try," he said.

"I have to find my boots before we head out to the cottage."

"We don't have to go to the cottage," he said. "We can sleep in my room. Or we've got three rooms left in the east wing. Take your pick."

Amelia hadn't seen the manager's quarters yet. She was curious about how Sam and Sarah lived day to day. "Your room," she said. "Definitely your room."

He led her through a door behind the reception desk and down a long, narrow hallway. The hall opened into a small apartment tucked into one corner of the east wing. It wasn't much more than a sitting room and three small bedrooms.

"Is Sarah here?" Amelia whispered.

Sam shook his head. "They took one of the empty rooms. Bigger bed."

"How big is your bed?"

Sam opened the door to his room and flipped on the lights. Slowly, Amelia stepped inside, and when she took it all in, she laughed. "Wow."

"Wow you're impressed or wow this is the most pathetic thing I've ever seen?"

"It looks like the masculine version of my room at my parents'. It's as if I never escaped adolescence. As far as I know, they still have a pink canopy on my bed."

"I should get rid of some of this stuff," he said. "You're the first woman I've ever brought here. Probably the last."

"Where do you take your women?" she asked.

"I own an inn. Twenty-six rooms. I have a wide choice."

"Right. I guess I should have guessed that." She crossed to a pair of shelves that held a crush of trophies. Amelia picked one up and examined it closely. "All State?"

"I was a pretty good baseball player in high school."

"Some of these are for track," she said.

"Hurdles. I was good at that, too."

There was so much she had yet to learn about him. She knew nothing of his past beyond what she could see in this room. They hadn't discussed former lovers and girlfriends. She thought he'd attended college, but had he said what he'd majored in?

Then there were the little day-to-day familiarities: his favorite flavor of ice cream, the way he drank his coffee, the brand of toothpaste he used. She knew all of this about Edward and yet their relationship had fallen apart. Would she spend years learning about Sam only to have the same thing happen? And who would she be then? Would she have turned herself into what Sam wanted and have never lived for herself?

There was one thing she was sure about. How he'd react to her touch, to a kiss, how his body felt against hers. All the quiet intimacies that were burned into her memory forever.

"I don't see any trophies for sex," she teased. "You're pretty good at that." She glanced over her shoulder and gave him a playful look. "Or were you a late bloomer?"

"Are we really going to talk about this?" Sam asked.

She turned and walked toward him. "We have to talk about these things," she said. "It's what people do to get to know each other."

"Does that mean we're going to try to have a relationship?" Sam asked.

"Maybe," she said. "But only if we're honest with each other and ourselves."

"What if we still can't make each other happy?" Sam asked.

"Then we'll deal with that as it comes. But you have to give me at least a chance. Can you do that, Sam? Can you give me a chance?"

Sam reached out and cupped her face in his hands, then he kissed her, his tongue tracing the crease of her lips until she opened beneath him. "How can I refuse you anything, Amelia?"

WEDDING DAY AT the Blackstone Inn went off without a hitch. From the morning breakfast to the simple ceremony, to the dinner and reception, all the details worked to make it a memorable occasion.

The following day included a late brunch before all the guests finally departed and were delivered safely to their train.

Once the inn was quiet, Sarah, James, Amelia and Sam decided to have a small celebration of their own. They cracked open the last of the champagne and gathered in front of the fire in the front parlor to congratulate themselves on a job well done.

Strangely enough, Sam had found nothing to criticize over the course of the past forty-eight hours. Between the four of them they'd handled every emergency that had popped up and with smooth efficiency. Adding two more people to the staff had changed the whole mood of the workplace. They'd had fun—and innkeeping hadn't been fun for him in a very long time.

"I have a toast to make," Sam said, holding up his glass. "To a very successful weekend. We couldn't have done it without the help of Amelia and James. I'm sure our ancestors wouldn't mind if I named you honorary Blackstones. Thank you, both."

Sarah threw her arms around James's neck and kissed him, falling into his lap and knocking over his champagne glass in the process. Sam winked at Amelia. Though he wanted nothing more than to kiss Amelia senseless, he was worried that once he started, he wouldn't be able to stop.

"I have a toast, too," James said. He pulled Sarah to her feet and held her waist until she settled herself. Then he dropped to one knee in front of her. A gasp slipped from each of them as the scene unfolded.

"Sarah Blackstone, I've loved you from the moment we met that first day in high school. I promised myself that if I ever managed to grab your attention for longer than a few seconds, I'd tell you how I felt. So, here goes."

Tears glistened in Sarah's eyes when she glanced over at Sam. He smiled and nodded to her.

"I think you're the most amazing woman I've ever met and I know I could make you happy for the rest of your life. So, I'd like the chance to do that, starting now. Sarah Blackstone, will you marry me?"

Sarah's eyes went wide and her jaw dropped open. "Really?"

James nodded, then laughed. "Oh, there's a ring, too." He reached into his pocket, pulled out a velvet-covered box and then opened it in front of her. A huge diamond twinkled from inside.

Sarah's hand trembled as she held it out while James slipped the ring on her finger.

"Yes," she said. "Yes, I'll marry you, James."

She dropped down to her knees and wrapped her arms around his neck, giving him an enthusiastic kiss. Once she'd finished with James, she stumbled over to Sam and hugged him. Amelia was next and Sam saw that she'd grown teary-eyed, as well.

Sam shook James's hand and congratulated him on a very romantic proposal. Though he'd often worried about his sister's choices when it came to men, Sam had no doubt that Sarah and James were a good match. Their courtship had been ridiculously short, but they were meant to be.

Sarah stared down at her ring and gave James a fierce hug. "Thank you for sharing this with us," she said excitedly to Sam and Amelia. "I can't imagine a more perfect proposal."

"Now you'll have your own wedding to plan," Amelia said.

"And I'll need you to help me," Sarah said. "Will you be my maid of honor?"

Amelia nodded, the tears flooding her eyes once more. She gave Sarah a hug. "Of course."

Sam accepted James's invitation to serve as best man and gave the handsome young plumber a hearty hug. The newly engaged pair made their excuses and said good-night, hurrying upstairs to the room they'd shared the previous night.

"That was sweet," Amelia said, sitting on the sofa. She curled her feet up underneath her and fixed her gaze on the fire. "I've always wanted a sister. I would have settled for a brother, too, but that didn't happen for me."

Sam sat and put his arm around her, tugging her close. "Do you know why your parents only had you?"

"I've speculated," she said, "but my mother would never tell me the truth. I did overhear the servants talking once and they said that my mother never wanted me. She never wanted children at all. My father had threatened to divorce her if she didn't provide an heir. Nine months later, I appeared."

"A happy bundle of joy."

"Whom she immediately placed in the care of a nanny. My father, of course, wanted a boy. That never happened. I believe my mother was happy I was the only one."

He reached out and took her hand, twisting her fingers through his before he pulled her wrist to his lips. He pressed a kiss against the pulse point and Amelia smiled. "It was always a bit lonely."

"And what about you? Did you and Edward talk about children?"

Sam watched an uneasy expression flit across her face. He immediately wanted to take the question back. It was too soon, too personal. "You don't have to answer that. It's none of my business."

"It's all right. We did talk about it. Edward wanted a big family. Secretly I didn't want children at all. That was one of the reasons I wanted to end it. I didn't want to be in the same situation as my parents."

"So, no children?"

Amelia took a deep breath and forced a smile. "I just never thought I'd be a good parent. I didn't exactly have the best role models. I barely spent any time with my parents when I was young. And when I was older, I only wanted to escape them." She gave him a heart-breaking look. "I should want to have children."

"I suppose it doesn't come naturally to everyone," Sam said.

"What about your parents?"

Sam didn't want to tell her the truth, but they'd promised to be honest with each other. "My folks were great. We grew up running the inn, running around town, playing along the river. Some people would call it idyllic."

She smiled. "Some people would insist mine was idyllic simply because my mother bought me anything I wanted and dressed me in designer clothes. It looked very lovely from the outside, but it wasn't like having a real mother."

"What about your father?"

"Oh, he was different. He wasn't around much, but when he was, he was at least affectionate. He used to hug me and kiss the top of my head. But only if I got good grades or did something commendable."

"Jeez, you are a mess," Sam said. "With a childhood like that, it's lucky you haven't become an ax murderer or a raving psychopath."

Amelia gave him a playful shove. "Thank you for all the support."

"No," he said, grabbing her arms and forcing her to face him. "Listen to me. I understand why you want to live your own life. You make your own future. Whatever you decide, Millie, you're going to make it happen."

She stared at him, her expression doubtful. "I can make anything happen?" she whispered.

"Anything," he said.

Amelia reached out and began to unbutton the crisp white shirt he wore. His tie was already loosened, but she brushed it aside to focus on his shirt. Sam watched through half-hooded eyes. He moaned softly when she pressed her lips to the center of his chest, soft flesh meeting hard muscle.

Sam raked his fingers through her tousled hair, gently tempting her to glance up at him. But she was determined to do exactly as she pleased, to take advantage of his nearly constant need for her.

When she reached his belt, she made quick work of the buckle and moved on to the zipper on his trousers.

Sam closed his eyes, his mind focused on the touch of her fingers, first smoothing over the fabric of his boxers, then reaching inside to wrap around his shaft.

When her lips closed over him, he tipped his head back, arching instinctively, aching for more. Her mouth was warm and damp, her tongue teasing at him until he was harder than he'd ever been before.

As she began to move over his tip, her fingers stroked in a gentle rhythm. It was easy to get swept away by the sensations coursing through him. Usually she didn't

take him to completion this way, but tonight Amelia
had different plans.

Moments of exquisite pleasure washed over him but
Sam tried to hold on to a bit of control, determined to
make this last as long as possible. He edged closer and
closer to release and Amelia allowed him, knowing as
he did that his orgasm would be incredibly powerful.

The fire cracked and popped, catching his attention for a moment. A tiny lapse in his control and his
body betrayed him. A surge of pleasure and then the
spasms struck so suddenly, so powerfully, that a deep
gasp exploded from his chest.

These pleasures had become a daily part of his life;
a delicious treat that he enjoyed morning, noon and
night. But the erotic indulgences required Amelia. In
less than twenty-four hours she'd be gone. Was he really prepared to live without her? He'd promised her
she could have her own life. But how could he offer
her that?

8

AMELIA STOOD AT the sink in the inn's kitchen the next day, staring out at the drifts of powdery snow. Though the snow had stopped during the night, the wind was still blowing, creating problems with the roads.

She pulled her cell phone from her pocket and dialed Vivian's number. Vivian usually got into the office before ten, but with the snow in Boston, it would be difficult to get around.

To Amelia's surprise, her boss picked up after one ring. "My wandering curator!" she cried. "How's it going out in the hinterlands? Have you secured that bed yet?"

"I have," Amelia said. "I just wanted to let you know I'm going to try to get back tomorrow, weather permitting. I'll call Steven with my estimated arrival time and ask if he'll help me unload the trailer. I also have some interesting new leads on silver and pewter pieces."

"Lovely," Vivian said. "I'll be looking forward to your return. And you may want to phone your mother.

She called me last night looking for you. I told her where you were. I hope that's not a problem."

Amelia winced. "No. I'll give her a call. I was supposed to put in an appearance at her Valentine's Day Ball for the Philharmonic. She's probably wondering why I didn't show."

"I wish your mother would focus some of her fundraising prowess on our little museum," Vivian said. "Perhaps you might ask her to throw a ball for us?"

"I'm afraid she has her pet causes, Vivian. I doubt that she'd want to help an organization that employs her only daughter and keeps me from reaching my full potential as a Boston socialite."

"Hmm. That's a shame. Well, darling, drive safely and I'll see you tomorrow."

"'Bye, Viv." Amelia switched off her phone and moved away from the window. Leaning back against the edge of the sink, she rubbed her forehead with the corner of her phone. Dealing with her mother was forever a trial. No matter what the occasion, she always left Amelia feeling silly and ungrateful. She could work magic with guilt and Amelia was her favorite target. But if Amelia was ever going to truly be independent, she'd need to stand up to her mother.

"Hey, there. What are you up to in here?"

She opened her eyes and smiled at Sam. His hair was tousled and his eyes were sleepy. There were moments when Amelia was overwhelmed by his frantic passion and other moments when his boyish charm could send her pulse racing.

"I thought I'd get a start on the pewter." Amelia

had spread the inn's collection of pewter across the large worktable in the center of the kitchen, sorting the pieces by type. "I need to photograph each piece."

He crossed the room and slipped his arms around her. "I can help," he said.

"No, that's all right. You can go relax."

"Sarah and James are sound asleep in the parlor," he said. "And they both snore."

Amelia giggled. "I guess they are made for each other," she said.

The four of them had exhausted themselves over the weekend, culminating with their own champagne party in front of the fire, a gathering that had spontaneously turned into an engagement party for Sarah and James.

"I'm going to try to leave tomorrow," Amelia said. "If the wind dies down tonight, I think the roads will be clear."

"I could drive you back," Sam offered. "Maybe spend a bit of time in Boston."

Though she'd thought about different scenarios for their future, she'd never really been able to picture Sam in Boston with her. He seemed so perfect here at the inn, amid all the townspeople of Millhaven who had known him for years and years. He just had to realize that for himself.

"I'll be all right," she said.

"I'm sure you will," Sam said. "But Sarah and James can handle the weekday guests. I'd kind of like to see your life in Boston, so when we're apart, I can imagine where you are and what you're doing."

"There's not much to see," Amelia warned him. "I

spend most of my time at—" She caught herself, swallowing her next words as something odd occurred to her. Was he afraid that she would return to Edward? She reached out and smoothed a lock of hair from his temple, allowing her fingers to linger. "What are you worried about?" she asked.

"I'm…worried you'll end up in a ditch somewhere."

"Sam, I'm going home to my job. I'm not going home to Edward."

"But you're going to see him," Sam said.

"Maybe. But only to put an end to it once and for all," she said. She smiled, shaking her head. "If you ever meet Edward, you're going to find it amusing that you were ever concerned about him. He's just so…well, he's nothing like you."

The weather had made it impossible to formulate any definite plans for her departure, but she figured tomorrow would probably be the most logical choice. The roads should be cleared; the bed was packed and ready to go. There was nothing keeping her here.

Except her heart, she mused. She and Sam had talked about what would happen…after. But Amelia wasn't sure she wanted to make plans. In truth, she needed to put some distance between them.

It was so easy to get wrapped up in the passion of the moment with him; hormones racing through her body and making her believe that she couldn't live without him. The whole week had been like a fantasy. And yet fantasies often withered in the light of the real world. She'd fought hard for her own life and that life was in Boston.

"Amelia?"

She looked up to find Sarah standing in the doorway. "Hi. You're awake."

"Someone is waiting for you at the front desk. She says she's your mother."

Amelia gasped. "My mother?"

"She came in a limo. And she looks really pissed. Do you want me to bring her in here?"

Amelia grabbed a towel and wiped her hands. "Yes, bring her in here." She began to pace, her nerves on edge. She hadn't talked to her mother in a few months. Whenever they spoke, the conversation turned into an advertisement for Edward and the benefits of making a good marriage.

She'd obviously seen the photo of Amelia in the *Globe*. No doubt she'd discussed her "problem daughter" with Amelia's father and they'd decided her behavior warranted a face-to-face meeting. So she'd called Vivian to find out where she was staying.

"I'd like to meet your mother," Sam said.

"This would not be the best time for that," Amelia replied, grabbing his arm. "Why don't you go into the parlor? If things are all right, I'll bring her in."

HER MOTHER SWEPT into the kitchen as if it were one of her perfectly decorated salons. She wore a size two Chanel suit in her favorite color—taupe—and a full-length mink that she usually saved for winter luncheons with her friends.

"Hello, Mother."

She crossed to Amelia and kissed both cheeks, clutching her gloves. "Darling. You look pale and thin."

Amelia bristled. She couldn't ever remember her mother paying her a genuine compliment. "Thank you, Mother. I do feel paler and thinner. Why are you here? I'm sure it's not to comment on my health."

Olivia Gardner Sheffield regarded her daughter with a cool eye. "I don't know. I assume only a serious illness would prompt behavior like this, Amelia. These awful pictures of you and some stranger in a bed. They've been all over the news. I thought you'd at least taken a respectable job and now I find out it requires you to do the most tasteless things."

"Mother, you're making more of this than you have to. It was a publicity stunt and nothing more."

"Nothing more? Why are you still here? Is there something going on between you and this man?"

Amelia got up and went to the sink, fetching a glass of water for herself. "That's none of your business."

"No? What about Edward? He's a part of our family. His parents are our oldest and dearest friends. How am I supposed to—"

"I'm in love," Amelia finally said. "With Sam Blackstone."

The moment the words slipped out of her mouth she knew they were the truth. The words had just come naturally, without thought, without fear.

"Oh, Amelia, don't be ridiculous. You've only just met this man. One does not fall in love in a week. Love takes time and respect and care. This is about...lust.

Plain and simple. He's an attractive man, but that will not pay the bills. And you'll see that once you're home."

She shook her head. "I'm not going home with you, Mother."

"Do you realize what's at stake here? I got a call from Edward's mother a few days ago. Edward has met someone, a woman from a wealthy Brazilian banking family. She's very interested in marrying him. He is ready, Amelia, and if it isn't you, it will be someone else."

Amelia waited for some strong reaction to the news but nothing came. The most she could muster was a brief sense of happiness for an old friend. "I'm glad," she murmured. "He deserves someone who will love him."

"Amelia, you have to realize that this will affect your inheritance. We can't in good conscience give you ten million dollars if you're going to choose so unwisely."

Amelia had never cared about the money before. She'd always seen it as a form of control. But now her thoughts had changed. This was money her grandfather had left her. Married or not, it was her inheritance and her parents shouldn't be able to keep it from her.

"I'm glad you mentioned the money. When I get back to Boston, I intend to look into my inheritance, Mother. After all, I've never seen anything in writing that expresses Grandfather's wish that I be married in order to have it. My cousins got their money when they turned twenty-five. Why would I have different requirements, Mother? Can you explain that?"

Her mother opened her mouth, then snapped it shut. Amelia knew she'd hit a nerve. Were her suspicions correct?

"I have a car waiting," Olivia said, giving Amelia a disdainful look. "Go get your things and you can ride home with me."

"I'm staying here, Mother. I'll be back in Boston tomorrow. I'm sure you'll have more to say to me. I can't guarantee that I'll want to listen."

"You were always a stubborn child," her mother said.

"No, I wasn't, Mother. I was a very compliant child. For a long time I was willing to marry a man I didn't love, just to please you. But now I know that I could never do that. I want a future with a man who stirs my passions and feeds my soul. I want to need him more than I need food or air. And when I'm living my last days, I want to be certain that I've been loved better and longer than any woman on earth."

"Well, that certainly is a nice little fantasy," Olivia said.

"It's not a fantasy, Mother. It can be real. Trust me on this. It is real."

Her mother slowly put her gloves on, then adjusted her mink coat, tugging the collar up around her neck. "I can only hope that you'll come to your senses once you get home to Boston." She strode toward the kitchen door.

"I wouldn't count on it," Amelia called.

She listened to her mother's footsteps against the

hardwood floors and winced as the front door slammed. A few seconds later Sam strode in.

"Are you all right?" he asked, crossing the room to take her hand.

Amelia nodded. "Fine." She glanced around. "I—I need to finish this inventory."

"Leave it," Sam said. "Go get yourself bundled up. I have a surprise for you."

"A surprise? What kind of surprise?"

"You'll like it, I promise."

He pulled her into his arms and kissed her, his lips soft and searching. It was the perfect thing to erase the memory of her mother's visit. Sam had an uncanny knack for giving her exactly what she needed.

There would be time enough later to appreciate all the bridges she'd just burned.

SAM INSTRUCTED AMELIA carefully on what to wear. While she was dressing, he went to organize her surprise.

The Blackstone Inn, over the course of the years, had acquired a number of carriages and sleighs that were kept in a small barn on the corner of the property.

It had been years since his grandfather had kept horses, but since the Blackstone carriages made appearances at each of three summer parades held in Millhaven, Sam had formed a partnership with an old friend and local horse breeder, Dan Wheeler.

Dan and Sam trained two horses each year to pull the carriages and the occasional sleigh. One of the horses, a gentle mare named Prissy, stood silently in front of the sleigh, the bells on the harness jingling as she angled her head to stare at Sam.

"She's all set," Dan said. "I took the sleigh for a spin and the snow is perfect on the roads. Packed and smooth. Just take it easy."

"I will," Sam said. "Thanks for doing this for me on such short notice."

"No problem," Dan said with a grin. "When romance calls, guys like us have to answer."

"I've got to pull out all the stops. She's leaving tomorrow."

"Time for some serious action," Dan said, nodding.

The front door to the inn opened and Amelia stepped outside. "I can't believe you're making me go out in the cold on my—" She stopped short the moment she saw the horse and sleigh.

"Dan, this is my...friend Amelia Sheffield. Amelia, this is Dan Wheeler. He's providing the horse."

Her gaze was still fixed on the horse as she approached. "Wow." She slipped her arm through Sam's. "I've never been on a sleigh ride."

"Well, hop on board," Sam said, pulling her along beside him. He spanned her waist with his hands and lifted her into the sleigh, then helped her settle the heavy lap robe over her legs. Dan held on to Prissy until Sam got into the sleigh and took the reins.

Sam clicked his tongue and gently slapped the reins against the horse's flanks. Prissy broke into a quick walk and then a trot as they headed out to the main road. The steel runners hissed softly beneath them and the clop of the horse's hooves echoed through the trees.

Instead of turning into town Sam took a different route down a quiet, less-traveled country road as the sun set behind them. Prissy took to her task with controlled energy.

"Thank you for this," Amelia said, resting her head on his shoulder.

"I want you to remember this night," he said. "How quiet and beautiful the woods are. I want you to remember how much you want me to kiss you."

When they reached the end of the road, the woods around them opened up to a view of the river. Though the sky was darkening, Sam could make out a few details around them made visible by the two carriage lamps, the flames flickering in the soft wind.

"I can't believe it's been just a week since we met," Amelia said. "It seems like we've known each other forever."

Sam pulled the horse to a stop, then turned to her, taking her hands in his. "We've talked a little bit about the future, but we haven't made any firm plans. I have one thing I need to do before you leave." He reached into his jacket pocket and pulled out an old velvet box.

Amelia gasped, her gaze darting between his face and the box. "Stop," she said, shaking her head. Her hand came down on his, resting softly and covering the box. "I don't want you to do this now."

"What do you think I'm doing?" Sam asked.

"What are you doing?" she asked.

"You first."

She cleared her throat. "I'd expect that's a ring," she said. "And I assume that you're going to propose."

"I do have a proposal," he said. "But I don't have a ring."

"Sam, it's not the right time. There's so much we have to figure out and this is all so wonderfully romantic and I'm not sure I'd be able to say no. So please—"

"I'm not going to propose marriage," Sam interrupted. "I was going to make a different kind of proposal."

Amelia frowned and Sam opened the small box. The light from the lantern was just enough to make out a beautiful, heart-shaped filigree locket on a fine chain. "This belonged to my great-great-great-grandmother."

"It's lovely," she said.

"My great-great-great-grandfather gave it to her when he went off to fight in the Civil War. They weren't married, but he didn't want her to forget him when he was gone." Sam smiled. "I don't want you to forget me, Amelia."

"How could I ever forget you?"

He removed his gloves and carefully fastened the chain around her neck, tucking it beneath her scarf. Then he bent close. "Don't forget any of this, Millie," he whispered. He cupped her face in his palm and kissed her lips. "Or this."

Amelia smiled. "I won't forget," she said, teasing at his tongue with hers.

"And you'll never forget this," he said, slipping his cold hand beneath her jacket and under her sweater to cup her breast.

"Cold," she murmured. "But nice."

"We don't have to stop. As long as we stay beneath

the lap robe, we'll be fine. I can guarantee you'll never forget getting naked in the middle of a snowy forest."

"You want me to take all my clothes off?" Amelia asked, her face etched with disbelief.

Sam nodded, a devilish smile curling his lips. "It's no fun unless you go all the way." He pulled the lap robe up around his neck and slipped out of his jacket. "Now you," he said.

Amelia never backed down from a challenge, especially one that had to do with sex, and he watched her wriggle out of her clothes. He reached for her beneath the lap robe. To his surprise, she'd also removed her sweater and unbuttoned her shirt.

"Now you," she whispered.

As they worked at each other's clothes, the air around them was still. Every now and then a branch laden with snow would crack and break, the sound like a gunshot echoing through the night. They twisted and struggled to remove the rest of their clothes, shielding their bodies from the freezing temperatures beneath the warmth of the thick blanket.

The cold seemed to heighten every sensation, and when she finally wrapped her cool fingers around his stiff shaft, Sam felt a delicious rush of warmth race through his body.

His hands skimmed over her body, tugging her close. How would he ever live without her? Sam had grown accustomed to having her in his bed, to waking up each morning to the feel of her body curled against his. He'd been free to touch her and kiss her at will, but that would all end tomorrow.

She ran her fingers through his hair. "I don't even feel the cold." She bent closer and kissed him, her warm breath clouding around their faces.

With a soft growl he slid down and pressed her legs apart. He pulled her lower, until the blanket was bunched around her shoulders. Then he disappeared beneath the lap robe. A few seconds later his tongue found the spot he knew so well. He parted the damp lips between her legs and found her clit, licking at it until she couldn't help but arch against his mouth.

Sam had learned to read her reactions over the past week. He knew when she was growing close to release and he could slow his pace to drag the tension out even further. He loved to make her wait so her release would be shattering. Sam needed that now, her complete and utter surrender.

She was gasping for breath, her fingers twisted in his hair. He didn't feel the pain. Instead he felt himself slowly climbing to his own release. She wasn't even touching him and he was flirting with the edge.

Sam waited as long as he could and then waited a little longer. When the first shudder rocked her body, he quickly grabbed her legs, yanking her against him, her legs hitched on his hips. In one fluid motion he plunged inside her.

Amelia cried out, then dissolved into deep spasms, her orgasm overwhelming her. Sam followed her a few seconds later, his chin raking against the soft flesh of her breasts as he held her close.

Every time they shared this deep and physical connection, Sam thought it couldn't get any better. But then it did. With each joining, their connection grew stronger, an invisible thread drawing them closer and closer. Just not close enough.

"Are you all right under there?"

Sam pushed the lap robe down until his face hit the cold night air. "I think so. How about you?"

She smiled. "I'm fine. I'm not cold at all."

"Me, either. Now we should do what I've heard the Swedish do after sex."

"What is that?"

"They throw themselves into the nearest snowbank." He grabbed her waist. "Come on, let's do it. It will be refreshing."

"It will be crazy," Amelia said, wriggling away from him. "You can go ahead if that's what you want to do, but I got undressed. That was daring enough."

"Okay," Sam said. "I'm just going to make it really quick. Just lift the blanket for a second, then pull it back." He counted down from three and slipped out from beneath the blanket.

Sam jumped out of the sleigh and into the snow beside the road. His body sank into the deep powder. At first he didn't feel the cold, but then it hit him suddenly, a million little pinpricks to his skin.

He jumped up and began to brush the snow off his naked body, then rushed back to the sleigh. But when he grabbed the edge of the blanket, Amelia shook her head.

"No way you're crawling under here while you're all wet," she said.

But he managed to wrest the blanket from her hand.

When he got underneath, he pulled her body against his and she screamed. But Sam covered her mouth with his, waiting until her gasps turned to laughter.

He kissed her, smoothing the hair back from her face. "See, that's not so bad," he murmured.

"You're freezing," she said, her naked body trembling. "You're a very bad boy."

"I know," he said. "But you like a bad boy."

"I like you," she whispered, leaning close. She nuzzled her face into the curve of his neck, hugging him tight until his body began to warm.

Sam gazed up at the starlit sky and realized he was happy. Through Amelia's eyes he saw Millhaven and the inn in a new light, one not shaded by his resentment.

Was this the life he wanted, though, if it didn't include Amelia?

AMELIA SNUGGLED DOWN into the soft quilts on the bed, pulling them up over her nose to fight off the early-morning chill. The first rays of dawn were lightening the windows in the stone kitchen and Sam was still sound asleep beside her, his naked body radiating enough heat to keep both of them warm in even the coldest conditions.

She nuzzled her face into his chest and inhaled, trying to commit his scent to memory. Right now, she felt as if she could recognize him in the middle of the darkest night. But her memories would fade. The conversations they'd shared would gradually escape her mind until she remembered only his most interesting turn of phrase or the dearest admission of affection. None of the little memories would survive.

When she'd arrived in Millhaven a week ago, she'd never imagined her visit would turn into a romantic relationship. She'd thought she'd pick up the George Washington bed and head back to Boston. But then everything had gotten complicated.

From the moment Amelia had moved out of her parents' home and walked away from her engagement to Edward, she'd had a very detailed plan. She'd just forgotten to include romance in her agenda.

Was it any wonder? After Edward, the last thing she'd wanted in her life was another man to please.

Her entire life had been spent trying to live up to someone else's expectations. Her earliest memory was a moment spent on her grandfather's lap as he'd lectured her on what it meant to be a Sheffield.

But a year ago she'd decided to live her life on her terms, to build a career and to start to dream of bigger things than just a solid society marriage and a bunch of entitled children, giving birth to just enough boys to take over the family business and enough girls to make important marriages.

She could understand Sam's unhappiness with taking over the family business. Like her, he'd also been saddled with expectations, unable to choose the life he wanted and yet refusing to share the burden with anyone who offered.

Amelia didn't want to end up in another dead-end trap. She loved Sam. She loved the inn. She could be making beds or washing dishes or dusting yet another

Federal-era table and the work seemed entirely satis-
fying.

But was she being honest? Would running the inn
with Sam be enough to fulfill her professionally? Or
was she just trying to convince herself of something
that she knew wasn't true? The only way to find out
was to leave.

She slipped her arm around him and snuggled
closer. Sam took a deep breath and opened his eyes,
pulling back to meet her gaze. "Morning, sunshine."

"Morning," Amelia said. She crawled on top of him
and stretched her body out over the length of his. As
she kissed him, she felt his shaft grow hard between
them, the heat branding her belly.

"Stop," he murmured, catching her wrists in his
grasp.

"What's wrong?"

"I can't do this," he said, rolling her over beneath
him. "Not this morning. I can't make love to you and
then just let you walk out the door and drive away. It's
not possible."

Sam tossed the covers aside and crawled out of bed,
his body unaffected by the chill in the air. He walked
over to the hearth and began to rebuild the fire. When
the flames engulfed the birch logs and illuminated
the dark room, he sat on the floor and stared into the
flames.

She watched as the light flickered over his bare skin,
his shoulders and arms outlined by a golden light. He
was more beautiful than any man she'd ever met. If
there was a perfect match for her, then Sam was as

close as she was going to get. Amelia looked down at the locket he'd given her the night before.

Once she'd had a chance to look at it in more detail, Amelia had realized how lovely it was. Exactly the kind of thing she'd have chosen for herself, a vintage setting with beautiful details. "Maybe it's like ripping off a bandage," she murmured.

"What?" He glanced over his shoulder.

"You're right. We shouldn't prolong the goodbyes. I should just pack up and go. The more we drag it out, the harder it will be."

"Yes," he said.

Amelia crawled out of bed and found a long-sleeved T-shirt draped over a nearby chair. She tugged it on before she realized it was Sam's shirt. It was soft and faded and felt great against her skin. Then she found her cardigan and pulled it on over top.

"That's not your shirt," he said.

"I'm appropriating it. If I can't sleep with you, then I'm going to sleep with this shirt. You can take whatever you like from my bag."

"Anything?"

She nodded. Sam got to his feet and picked up her bag from the upholstered bench at the end of the bed. He pulled open the zipper and began to dig through the contents.

"What are you looking for?" she asked.

"I'll know when I find it."

Eventually he pulled out her shampoo, untwisted the top and took a deep breath. "Apples," he said. "Your hair smells like fresh apples."

"Are you going to sleep with my shampoo?"

"No," Sam said. "I'm going to wash my pillowcases in it and then I can pretend you're in bed with me."

Amelia grabbed her cell phone, selected the camera app and snapped a photo of him looking all dark and moody. "You could also take a photo." She took another picture of Sam, then admired it, especially the naked butt.

He chuckled and turned around. "Give me that!"

She quickly snapped another shot before he could grab the phone and look at it. "Now you," he said. "Lie back."

Amelia smiled at him and he pressed the button on her phone. He stared at the picture for a long time before nodding. "Perfect," he murmured. He punched in his number and sent the photo to his phone.

Meanwhile, Amelia found a pair of yoga pants and tugged them on. She dressed for warmth and comfort and added a pair of thick socks and her boots. When she was finished, she picked up a few of her belongings still in the adjoining bathroom and tucked them into her overnight bag.

He watched her from the bed, his gaze silently following her every move. She felt his eyes on her like a sweet caress. She returned to the bed and sat down.

"Are you going to be all right here on your own?"

He smiled. "Probably not. I'm planning to take to my bed and mope around for the next few weeks."

She reached out and cupped his face with her palm. "Please don't do that. When I think of you, I'd like to think that you are happy."

It was a sweet sentiment, but one that Sam wasn't ready to accept. He wanted her to stay. Amelia could see it in his eyes. But she'd already decided that she had to go home.

She had to put their relationship in perspective. She couldn't seem to think rationally when she was around him. The magnetic pull between them was too strong to deny. When she was with him, she was ready to throw everything she'd built in the past year away. She had to be sure that would truly make her happy. Her feelings for Sam defied any and all reason. They lived two different lives in two different places. Their physical attraction seemed much too powerful to sustain over time. And though they shared a few interests, Amelia wasn't sure what his hobbies were—beyond sex with her.

She lay across his naked chest, her cheek pressed against the smooth muscle. His heart beat, slowly, steadily, and Amelia closed her eyes. It would be so simple to stay here with him, to just abandon her job and her life and make a new one with Sam.

"Tell me what's going to happen now," Amelia murmured. "Will you call me? Will I call you? Will we just wait to see who gives in first?"

He smoothed his hand over her hair. "Why don't you call me when you get home, just so I know you're safe? And then we'll go from there."

"When will we see each other again?"

Sam thought about this a bit longer. "When do you want to see each other again?"

"I'm probably going to want to drive back here

next weekend. But I'm not sure that would be the best thing."

"Does absence make the heart grow fonder?" Sam asked. "Because I can't imagine my heart being any fonder of you than it already is."

Amelia dropped a kiss on his lips. "I'm awfully fond of you, too, Sam Blackstone." She glanced at the clock on the bedside table. "I should probably get on the road."

He groaned, pulling her close, but Amelia wasn't going to get caught up in any long and emotional good-byes. They'd decided to see each other again, so there was no need to get all sappy about her departure.

"I refuse to get sentimental," Amelia said. "I'm just going to say goodbye."

He shook his head. "I think that's best," Sam said. He sat up, the sheets falling away from his naked chest. Her gaze dropped to the smooth expanse of chiseled muscle and hard flesh. "I'm not going to tell you how much I'll miss you. Or how I won't be able to sleep without you by my side."

"Stop," Amelia warned.

"Or how I'll miss the feel of your hands on my body or the taste of your lips on mine."

"You're deliberately trying to make this difficult."

"I'm trying to ensure that you'll remember what we shared here," Sam said. "So maybe you'll want to come back."

"I really don't want to leave," she said softly.

He pulled the blankets back. "Then come to bed, Millie."

"I can't. But I promise I will be back."

"Soon?"

She nodded, then went to pick up her overnight bag. "Stay warm without me, Sam," she said.

"I'll be thinking of you," he said, smiling.

She crossed the room and leaned over the bed, giving him one last kiss. It was sweet and perfect and Amelia closed her eyes as she pulled away. Then, with one last look at him, she turned and walked out of the stone kitchen.

Amelia threw her bag into the back of the Lexus and hopped in behind the wheel. For a moment, before she pushed the ignition, she hoped that it wouldn't start, that she'd have another excuse to stay. But the engine roared to life in the quiet morning air.

She was just about to pull out when she saw Sarah hurrying from the inn, a basket in her arms. The other woman opened the passenger's-side door and placed the basket on the seat. "Just a little something for the trip," she said. "Coffee and some pastries and fruit. And some of that granola that you like. Oh, and left-over quiche."

Amelia reached over and gave Sarah's hand a squeeze. "Thank you," she said.

"You're coming back, right? He won't be able to do without you."

"And what about you?" Amelia asked. "I'm going to be your maid of honor. You can come to Boston to look for wedding dresses. We'll make a weekend out of it."

Sarah smiled. "Goodbye, Amelia."

"See you, Sarah. Take care of him."

As she steered the SUV out onto the road, Amelia took one last look at the Blackstone Inn. When she'd arrived in Millhaven, she'd come for nothing more than an old bed. And now that she was departing, she was leaving behind something entirely unexpected. A man. A man who might be her future.

9

SAM HUNG UP the phone, then rubbed his tired eyes with the heels of his hands. Suddenly he felt utterly exhausted, as if he could crawl into bed and sleep for the next month.

"Are you going to mope for the rest of your life or are you going to go to Boston and try to convince Amelia to come back and live here with us?"

Sam glanced up and gave Sarah a cold look. "I'm not moping. And she's only been gone for six hours. I'm not that pathetic that I can't do without her for that long."

"What's with the sad-puppy face, then?" she asked.

"There's nothing wrong with my face."

"James, does Sam have a sad-puppy face? Be honest."

Sam glanced over at James, who'd just wandered into the room, his toolbox in one hand and a crescent wrench in the other. Sam's eyebrow arched as he waited for James's answer.

"I'm not getting in the middle of this," James finally

said. "I've decided to make that rule number one. I'm going to go install that new water filter instead."

James walked out of the room, leaving Sarah and Sam to discuss family matters in private. "We're getting a water filter?" Sam asked.

Sarah nodded. "He had one sitting around and thought he'd install it in the kitchen. He's determined to modernize our plumbing. I told him he could do it as a wedding present to me."

"Wedding presents already?" Sam said. "You just got engaged."

Sarah stared at him for a long moment. "So, are we going to talk about her or are we just supposed to forget that Amelia ever existed?"

"No, we can talk about her," Sam said. In truth, Sam needed to talk about her. It made her seem more real. "I told her I understood how much her independence meant to her. So I have to let her go home. We need some time apart to see if we really want to be together. It makes sense. Not all of us fall in love in a matter of days like you and James."

"James and I have known each other for years. And people fall in love at first sight all the time."

"And that's you. You've only been madly in love for…what? Three days?"

"Actually, it's been a little longer," Sarah admitted. "He was here a couple months ago to install the new toilet in the stone kitchen. That's when I decided there might be something between us. The point is, I didn't let anything stand in my way. Don't be such a wuss, Sam. Go after her."

"The last thing I want is to show up on her doorstep and get shut down. She knows my life is here, not in Boston. That doesn't leave us many options."

"How did you leave it?" Sarah asked.

"I'm not sure. It was all a little vague. She did accept the locket I gave her."

"You gave her a *locket*?" Sarah asked, her voice laced with disbelief. "What kind of gift is that? What's that supposed to mean? A locket? Twelve-year-old boys give their girlfriends lockets."

"It wasn't just any locket. It was great-great-great-grandmother's locket. The silver one with the filigree setting. She liked it."

"So you want her to come back," Sarah said.

"Sure. But she has a life in the city. What do I do if she wants to stay there?"

"You go there and try to make it work," Sarah said.

"I have an inn to run," he said.

"James and I can run the inn. He loves the place. It makes him excited. There are just so many things to fix. This morning he spent two hours making lists of all the things that needed to be done here. He made me dig through old bills and records to find out when the roof was last fixed and when the electrical was overhauled. The question is, do you want to run the inn?"

Sam realized he'd made that decision last night in the sleigh. "Yes, but only with Amelia."

She reached into her pocket. "I found this old brochure. It has a bunch of information about the George Washington bed. It's from the bicentennial in 1976.

You might want to give a copy to Amelia. That would give you an excuse to call her."

She held out the brochure to Sam and he took it, then crossed the room to the sofa and sat to read it. But as he stared at the photo on the cover, Sam recognized the bed in the cover picture. It was sitting in room twelve, the room that Amelia had stayed in her first night at the inn.

"Oh, hell," he murmured. "It's the wrong bed. She's got the wrong damn bed."

Sarah sat beside him on the sofa. "What are you talking about?"

"This is a photo of the George Washington bed. Taken about forty years ago. Notice anything?"

"That's not the bed you gave to Amelia."

"It's not," he said.

"So which bed is the real bed?" Sarah asked.

"I'm beginning to wonder if there really is a George Washington bed." Sam shook his head. "What if this was all some marketing trick made up by one of our great-great-great-grandfathers?"

"George Washington did stay at the inn," Sarah said. "We have his signature in the guest book on three different dates."

"Sure, and maybe when the inn suffered a few financial setbacks, the Blackstone ancestor-in-charge chose a bed, claimed it was the one that George Washington slept in and sold it to some unsuspecting collector. It would be a quick way to put the books back in the black." He chuckled softly. "Not a bad plan," he said.

"Except you gave the bed to Amelia."

"I gave *a* bed to her." He waved the brochure. "And according to this, we still have the authentic bed. At least the bed that was authentic in 1976."

"What if they find out the truth about the bed?" Sarah said. "Do you think she could lose her job?"

"She didn't pay for it. I can't imagine that it would cause a problem."

Sarah shrugged. "Yeah. But people are paying to see the bed. Wouldn't that be…"

"Fraud?" Sam asked. Sarah did have a point. "I don't want to get her into trouble. I can pack up the other bed and drive it to Boston and—"

"If you leave later in the afternoon, then maybe she'll ask you to spend the night." Sarah slid over and threw her arms around her brother's neck. "I love you, big brother. Don't let her get away."

He tucked the old brochure into his shirt pocket and walked up the stairs. When he reached the room at the end of the hall, he opened the door and entered. He hadn't been in the room since the first night he'd met Amelia. The first night he'd kissed her.

He looked at the flowers he'd picked for her, now a little wilted and standing in a glass vase. Such a strange set of circumstances had brought him and Amelia together. A silly old bed. Was this the fates at work? Was the universe conspiring to bring them together again?

Sam didn't want to appear desperate to see her. And he didn't want her to think he was making excuses to check up on her. He'd decided five minutes after she'd driven away that she'd need to come back to him.

But maybe he ought to just call her and give her the

option of having him deliver the bed or send it another way. The last thing he wanted to do was to make her think he didn't respect her independence.

Life had a funny way of throwing a wrench into a guy's plans, even when he didn't have any plans at all. He'd been waiting for his life to begin, angry that he'd been tethered to the inn and helpless to choose his own happiness.

When Amelia had walked in, it was as if a switch had been thrown. He could suddenly imagine a future, and a happy future at that. But only if it included working side by side with Millie.

So he would give her a choice. If she wanted to live in Millhaven, he'd make her an equal partner in the inn. If she wanted to stay in Boston, he'd do whatever it took to be with her. He could be digging ditches, shoveling sand, picking rocks from a field. As long as he had Amelia waiting at home for him, he'd be happy.

Yes, he needed to see her again. He needed to say all those things that he'd left unsaid. He had to convince her that her life was with him, wherever that might be.

He couldn't offer her a prestigious job in the art world or the kind of career she'd dreamed of. He couldn't give her an apartment overlooking Boston harbor and an exciting slate of social activities. But he could give her days full of laughter and nights full of passion.

If Amelia was the kind of woman who wanted something like that, then maybe she'd accept his proposal. He crossed to the bed and began to tear the sheets off.

Hearing the noise, Sarah appeared in the doorway. "Do you need some help?"

He grinned at his little sister. "Yeah, I could use a hand."

"I want you to bring her back," she said. "She belongs here with us. And she could never be happy anywhere else."

"I hope you're right," Sam replied. "And I don't know whether anything I say will work. She wanted to go back. She's proud of her job."

"Just tell her that you love her," Sarah said. "Everything will fall into place after that."

"If it were only that simple," Sam murmured.

AMELIA GOT BACK to the city around 10:00 a.m., and considering the weather, the trip had been uneventful. The interstate had been lined with tall mounds of snow. Safe inside the inn, she hadn't realized how bad the storm had been.

The miles were passed listening to sappy country love songs and punctuated by quiet sobs and soft laughter. She'd relived every single moment she'd spent with Sam, trying to remember their conversations word for word and failing miserably.

When she got to Boston, though everything looked familiar to her, it didn't feel comfortable or soothing, the way home should. Instead she found herself longing for the quiet, warm atmosphere of the inn and for the man who lived there.

The farther away she got from Sam, the more she felt the pull of their connection. Three hours seemed like nothing, and yet it felt as far away as the moon. It wasn't just the physical distance but the act of leaving each other, of giving up what they'd shared for the responsibilities of the outside world.

The traffic in downtown Boston was tricky. The narrow streets were lined with parked cars and the pedestrians were crossing against the lights. When she reached the Mapother, she pulled her SUV and the trailer into the loading dock.

Amelia had never really learned to maneuver the trailer in reverse, so she hopped out and walked to the security entrance right beside the tall garage doors. She slid her security card against the sensors and entered.

Mike Parris, the head of shipping and receiving, was passing by and he stopped. "Hey there, Amelia. Did you get your bed?"

Amelia smiled. "I did. It's outside in the trailer. Can you have someone unload it and get it up to the exhibit? We open next Monday and I need to get everything finished this week. We've got school groups coming on Friday and it would be nice to preview it for them."

"No problem," Mike said. "I'll deal with the trailer." He paused. "Oh, by the way, Vivian was looking for you. She's been asking about you all morning. You might want to check in with her."

"I was hoping to go home and grab a quick shower. Is she just casually looking or does she seem desperate to find me?"

"On a ten-point scale, I'd say her desperation is about a fourteen and rising."

Amelia smiled. "All right." She gave Mike her keys,

then headed through the warren of racks and storage areas to the office. As she passed her own office, she grabbed the stack of pink phone messages that had been left on the corner of her desk.

She found her boss three doors down in an office piled with books, magazines and empty Starbucks cups. "I'm back. They're unloading the bed right now. It should be ready for previews by Friday."

Vivian motioned to her, pointing to a chair across from her desk. "Come in, Amelia. I trust you had a pleasant trip back?"

"The roads were a bit slippery in spots, but I didn't have any trouble. I did run into a few problems with the bed. We've only got it on loan. There wasn't a clear bequeath to the museum, so I had to settle for what I could get."

"Well, darling, you've done a wonderful job for us here at the Mapother. You've always been willing to go the extra mile, if you know what I mean." She cleared her throat. "And I certainly don't regret hiring you, but…"

A sick feeling washed over Amelia and she stared at Vivian in disbelief. "Are you firing me?"

"Darling, *firing* is such a harsh word. I'd prefer to say we're parting ways."

"Why? I got the bed. Granted, it took me a bit longer than anticipated, but it's here and it's ready for the exhibit opening next week. You said it was all right for me to take the time."

"This has nothing to do with your exhibit, which I'm sure is going to be a great success."

"What is it, then?"

"We've received a rather substantial donation. Five million in cash. Our largest single donation ever."

"Well, what does that have to do with me?"

"The donation came with a condition. If we want the money, we have to end our relationship with you."

"I don't understand. If we have more money, we shouldn't be cutting staff."

"Darling, the money is coming from your family's foundation. They asked that we terminate our professional relationship with you."

Suddenly everything became perfectly clear. Amelia had suspected that her mother was ruthless when it came to getting what she wanted and this proved it.

"Your mother said there might be more for us, depending upon…"

"Oh, I understand now," Amelia said. "She's decided to punish me the only way she knows how. It's quite a clever idea, if I do say so myself."

"Amelia, you have to understand our point of view. We can't turn down that kind of money. The board would fire me in a heartbeat if I did. We all have to make sacrifices for things we believe in. I happen to believe the Mapother needs this money."

"What am I supposed to do now? I guess there won't be any letter of recommendation, either."

Vivian leaned forward and lowered her voice. "I have a friend who works for a small decorative arts museum in San Francisco. She has a job for you if you want it. It pays better than the Mapother. It's actually a promotion for you. Take advantage of this change, Amelia, and I think you'll come out on top."

Amelia looked up at her boss and forced a smile. Vivian had taken a chance on her when no one else would. She owed her for that at least. "Thank you. I'll look into San Francisco."

"It's called the San Coronado," Vivian said. "It's lovely. Spanish architecture, red-tiled roof. And it's right along the ocean. Couldn't be a prettier setting."

Amelia nodded as she walked to the door. "I'll just get my things together. I won't be long."

"Darling, take your time. It's the least we can do for you."

Amelia walked through the offices, past her coworkers. She was numb, as if a bomb had gone off beside her. She couldn't hear; she couldn't speak. She felt angry and humiliated and so very sad. Amelia loved her job and now someone else would do it.

"Amelia! Welcome back."

She turned to smile at Serena Phillips, the head of their communication department. "Thanks."

"We're still getting calls about your sleep-in," she said. "Lots of great press on that. Brilliant move."

By the time she reached the Lexus, her eyes were burning with tears. She'd known her mother was capable of cruelty, but she never truly believed it would be directed at her.

Thankfully the trailer had been unhitched and her SUV was parked in its usual spot, the keys inside. She sat in her vehicle for a long moment, wondering what her next move should be.

Every instinct told her to drive right back to Mill-haven. Sam was there. He'd offer comfort and security, a place to stay until she got her life sorted out. Her second instinct was to visit the family lawyer. The money she'd been promised in her grandfather's trust was not something her parents could just give away on a whim. Somehow, she sensed that she was being played and that all was not what it seemed.

Instead Amelia decided to go home. She'd confront her mother one last time, then cut ties with her altogether. She steered the SUV through city traffic, thinking about all the things she wanted to say.

Amelia tried to see the situation from her mother's viewpoint. Amelia was her only child. But why try to force that child into being something she wasn't? Couldn't her mother just accept her as she was instead of trying to change her?

She pulled up in front of her parents' townhome on Beacon Hill. They usually spent the week in town, then headed out to their weekend home on Cape Cod. It was morning and her mother would be going through her week's schedule, accepting luncheon invitations, making plans to play tennis with her friends, arranging shopping trips and meetings with the household staff.

The last person she'd expect to see would be Amelia. Or maybe she was waiting, hoping that she'd get a chance to savor her victory. She'd managed to destroy the last of her daughter's happiness.

Amelia still had a set of keys for the house, so she parked in the back, in her father's spot. The security system beeped as the door opened. Amelia walked through the silent house. She found Inez, their housekeeper, in the library. "Hello, Inez. I'm looking for my mother."

"Miss Amelia. How lovely you look today."

"Thank you. I'm looking for my mother."

"She hasn't come down yet. Let me go up and tell her you're here. I'm sure she'll want to see you."

She took a seat in one of her father's leather wing chairs, uncertain of what kind of reception she'd get. Certainly her mother wouldn't expect her to be happy. She clenched her hands, trying to release the tension in her body. When that didn't work, she got to her feet and began to pace.

"Hello, Amelia."

She spun around to face her mother, who stood in the doorway to the library. "Hello, Mother."

"What brings you here? You haven't set foot in this house in…what? A year?"

"It's a long time for parents to be estranged from their only child."

"I'm not sorry for what I did, Amelia. I needed to make you come to your senses. I'm sure eventually you'll come to forgive me and forget this little…bump in the road. I only want what's best for you."

"No, Mother, you want what's best for you. You don't care about how I feel. You don't care what makes me happy."

"That's not true."

"I loved my job. I was proud of the work I was doing."

"You'll get over it."

"I loved my life. I was independent. I wasn't afraid of anything. I had a future."

"You can still be happy," her mother said.

"Happy? Like you're happy? Your marriage is nothing more than a business arrangement. You sleep in separate bedrooms and I don't think I've seen Father kiss you since I was a kid. Your friends don't care about you, they care about your money. You don't trust anyone and you even can't bring yourself to love your only child. The years are passing you by, Mother, and look at what your life has become. Don't you want to be happy?"

"That's not always possible," Olivia said, her expression cold. "I do my best with what I've been given— including an ungrateful daughter."

"I'm not ungrateful, Mother. I'm just finished. You can officially kick me out of the family. You don't have to worry about me anymore. I'm relieving you of your responsibility."

"Don't be silly. You can't walk away."

"Watch me. Sam showed me what love is supposed to be. I was afraid I would allow myself to be controlled, like you tried to control me. But now I know how strong I am and what I truly want. You can keep your money. You can't do anything more to me."

Amelia got up and turned to walk out. But she froze

when she saw Edward standing in the doorway. Amelia glanced back at her mother. "You are cruel," she said.

Taking a deep breath, she walked to the door and smiled up at Edward. She took his hand and led him through the house and out the door to the small garden. As was everything else in Boston, it was covered with snow.

"Do you mind if we walk?" Edward asked. "It's easier to stay warm."

"Sure," she said.

They walked out to the street and strolled down the narrow sidewalk. "How did you know I was here?" she asked.

"Your mother suspected you'd be coming by this morning. Inez called me right after you arrived." He shook his head. "Don't blame her. She was only following orders."

"Edward, I know that you've always wanted things to be different between—"

Edward pressed a finger to her lips. "Stop. Let me talk."

"All right," she said, his fingers still on her lips.

"You were right," Edward said.

"I was?"

He nodded. "We were a good match, but not a great match. I thought it was enough to be good together. Until I met Vanessa."

"Vanessa?"

"Vanessa. She works in our securities division. Vanessa Paredes. She's from Argentina."

"Argentina?"

"Yes. She's beautiful and fiery and funny and passionate and we are perfect for each other. If it weren't for you, I never would have found her."

Amelia threw her arms around Edward's neck and gave him a fierce hug. "I'm so happy for you."

"And I'm happy for you," Edward said. He stepped back. "There is one more thing, Amelia. Something you should know."

"What is it?"

"Your grandfather's trust," he said. "Your parents were using it to try to get you to marry me. And, for a while, I supported that effort. But they don't have any right to keep that money from you. It's yours." He reached into his breast pocket and pulled out his business card. "Call me. I can help you get it."

She looked down at the card, tears swimming in her eyes. "Thank you, Edward."

He leaned close and kissed her cheek. "I'll send you an invitation to the wedding."

"I wouldn't miss it," Amelia said.

She watched him walk away, the collar of his cashmere overcoat pulled up against the wind. A shiver skittered through her and she rubbed her arms through her down jacket.

Amelia glanced up and down the street. What was next? she wondered. For the first time in her life there were no expectations hanging over her head. And, for the first time in her life, Amelia knew exactly where she belonged.

A LIGHT SNOW began to fall right around sunset. The radio forecasters predicted another snowstorm, this time moving in from the west.

Sam had made the drive to Boston faster than his map program told him he could, but the trip hadn't turned out anything as he'd expected.

He started at the museum, certain that he'd find Amelia hard at work when he arrived. But the museum was closed to visitors until noon. When he went to the loading dock, a security guard informed him that they couldn't take his shipment without an approved bill of lading. Sam asked to talk to Amelia, but the guard told him that Ms. Sheffield was no longer employed by the museum.

Sam didn't know what the hell to make of that news, so he decided to forget the element of surprise and call her. But when he dialed her cell phone number, there was no answer. He had her home address and decided to try that next. But after hanging around in front of her building for two hours, and buzzing at half-hour intervals, she didn't respond and her apartment appeared dark and deserted.

What the hell had happened? He tried to formulate some possibilities and the only thing he could come up with was that she was with her family. Maybe she'd decided to go home to make amends with her parents. Or maybe Edward had been the lucky guy to warrant a visit.

"Damn it, Amelia," he muttered. "What the hell is going on?"

Sam grabbed his cell phone again, this time dialing

the inn. Sarah picked up after two rings. "Blackstone Inn. This is Sarah."

"Hey, it's me," he said.

"Hey, you! How's it going? Is Amelia with you? Let me talk to her."

"She isn't. I wasn't able to find her. Something is going on. I was wondering if she might have called the inn."

"No. What do you think is wrong?"

"They said she didn't work at the museum anymore."

"What does that mean?" Sarah asked.

Sam swore beneath his breath. "I don't know." He paused to gather his thoughts. "I even drove past her parents' house."

"Did you go in?"

"No, there was a gate. If she's there, she doesn't need me interrupting her. Besides, I'm not ready to meet her parents."

"What are you going to do?" Sarah asked.

"I'm coming home," he said.

"What about the bed?"

"The museum has the wrong bed. But since she doesn't work there anymore, I suppose it doesn't make a difference."

"You're giving up awfully easy," Sarah said.

"It was a bad idea in the first place. This is just the fates telling me it wasn't meant to be."

"I wouldn't be so sure of that," Sarah insisted.

"She left this morning," he said. "If she had really wanted to stay, she would have."

"But you're in love with her," Sarah said.

Sam sighed heavily. "I guess I am."

"I'll see you in a little while," Sarah said. "I'm cooking roasted chicken for dinner. James is eating with us."

Sam flipped off his phone and tossed it on the passenger seat. He'd need to get used to being the third wheel at the inn. No doubt, James would be moving in soon. And though it would be nice to have a handy guy around, living with a third person would be an adjustment.

He'd imagined how things might end with Amelia, but he'd never pictured this. He'd gone from holding her in his arms that morning to wondering where she was and who she was with twelve hours later.

Edward. That was the only name that was banging around in his head at the moment. But why? He knew Amelia didn't love him, and yet Sam still felt threatened. Maybe it was because Sam knew what he'd do to keep Millie in his life. If Edward felt even half for her as much as Sam did, he wouldn't let her out of his sight. And the other man had much more to offer.

Sam reached for the radio and switched it on to a country station as he headed home, listening to song after song about betrayal and heartbreak.

He didn't regret a single moment of his time with her. He'd put it all out there, risked everything, opened his heart as he never had before. If she was gone for good, he'd accept the fact and move on.

Yet Sam couldn't imagine what it might be to start another relationship with someone new. He was twenty-eight years old. He'd had a number of lovers and girlfriends in his life but not one of them had compared to Amelia. Not one of them had captured his heart as she had.

So he'd spend the rest of his life alone. At least now he could appreciate the inn and all its quirks.

But what if Amelia had quit her job so that she could come back to Millhaven and be with him? That would mean all her intentions from that morning had fallen away. That she couldn't live without him. That she loved him as much as he loved her.

The thought occupied his mind as he finally drove through Millhaven and headed up the road to the inn. But to his disappointment, there was no Lexus SUV parked in the driveway when he arrived.

Sam parked his pickup near the kitchen door. The lights inside were on and he saw Sarah moving around through the frost-glazed windows. He opened the door and walked inside, stomping the snow from his boots.

Sarah was standing by the sink, a dish towel in her hands, when he came in. "Hey, there," she said.

"Hi," Sam said.

She crossed the room and wrapped her arms around him in a sisterly embrace. "You'll be fine. I promise. This will all work out."

"Have you picked up fortune-telling?" he asked.

"Yes," she said. "And my crystal ball indicates you have nothing to worry about."

Sam turned to the refrigerator and pulled out a beer. "For now, I'm going to toast my bachelorhood, I'm going to eat too many greasy snack foods and I'm going to watch hockey. If that doesn't make me feel like a man again, I don't know what will."

She picked up a plate with a piece of apple pie on it. "We have a guest. Can you take this into the dining room for me? I want to finish up these dishes. James is taking me bowling tonight."

Sam chuckled. "Maybe I'll forget the hockey and watch you bowl."

"Someone needs to stay with our guest. For tonight, that's your job."

Sam shrugged. "No problem." He grabbed the plate and headed toward the dining room, a beer in the other hand and a bag of potato chips tucked under his arm.

AMELIA GLANCED AT her watch. With every minute that passed she grew more anxious. Her drive to Millhaven had been fraught with doubt and indecision. But somehow, deep inside her heart, she knew it was right to come back. There were things she needed to say, things that couldn't be said over the phone.

When she'd arrived at the inn, she'd expected he'd be there. But instead she found Sarah and James in the midst of baking apple pies for the week's guests. Sarah didn't seem to be surprised to see her and she welcomed her in. Unfortunately Sam had left earlier in the afternoon with a long list of errands for the inn.

Amelia had hoped for the element of surprise, but after waiting for almost three hours, she was worried that Sam wasn't going to return at all. When she noticed headlights through the dining room windows, Amelia held her breath and slowly let it out when she recognized Sam's truck.

She'd had plenty of time to figure out what she

wanted to say. First she'd thought she'd be cute and ask for a job as a chambermaid. Then she figured it was best to just throw herself in his arms and kiss him and let passion rule the day. Finally she'd decided on a heartfelt admission of her love for him and a promise that she wanted to begin a life together immediately.

With a shaky hand, she took a long sip of her water. But when she set it down, the glass tipped over, spilling water off the edge of the table and onto her lap. With a soft curse, Amelia stood and brushed the water off her with her napkin. And it was this way that Sam found her as he came out of the kitchen.

"Amelia?"

She looked up at him and forced a smile. This wasn't going to go according to plan at all. "Hello, Sam."

He stood frozen for a long moment, staring at her, a plate of pie in his hand. "Wha— What are you doing here?"

"Waiting for you," she said, tossing the napkin on the table. Though it had been about only twelve hours since they'd seen each other last, it seemed like days. And it felt as if she were talking to a stranger.

Maybe if she touched him, that strange sensation would go away. But if she touched him, he'd see how her hand trembled and he'd know how scared she was. Instead she clutched her hands in front of her. "I've come to ask for a job. I'm afraid I don't come with references. I got fired from my last job just this morning. But I'm a hard worker and I learn fast and I won't give you a bit of trouble."

He smiled. "You're asking me for a job?"

Amelia shrugged. "That was my first option. Why don't you let me try my second?"

He set down the stuff in his hands, pulled out a chair and sat. "Go ahead. I'm listening."

"This isn't exactly a listening option." Amelia slowly crossed the room, bent close and then kissed him, her lips soft against his, her tongue teasing at the crease of his lips.

Sam slipped his fingers through her hair and pulled her closer, lingering over the kiss for a bit longer than she'd intended.

Her heart slammed in her chest and her breath came in quick gasps. Sam seemed to enjoy the kiss, but then, he always had.

"Option three," she said, holding up three fingers.

"Can we go back to two for a little while? I'm not sure I got enough of that to make an informed decision."

"Option three," Amelia insisted. "I realized shortly after I left this morning that I was making a huge mistake. I was afraid that my love for you was too strong, that it would undo all the work I've done over the past year. But I realized today that I'm stronger than that." She paused, taking a deep breath. "I'm in love with you. I think I have been from the very moment we met. I just couldn't leave that unsaid. I love you, Sam. I love you. I know it's kind of crazy and I've been trying my best not to—"

He stopped her words with his lips, pulling her into a fierce embrace. She stumbled backward and ran into the edge of a table, upsetting the glasses on top. It was as if they'd been apart for years, the kiss desperate with desire and longing. And when they finally pulled apart, they were both breathless.

Sam looked down into her eyes and chuckled softly. "I spent the day in Boston trying to find you," he murmured. "Now I know where you were."

"I had a very bad homecoming. I got fired and I told my mother off for the last time. And I broke it off completely with Edward."

"So you decided to come back here where life is so much simpler?"

She nodded. "I've been happy here with you. For the first time in my life, I'm in love. I know that now. It just took me a while to figure it out."

"I guess we're both a little slow on that subject," Sam said. He smoothed the hair away from her face and kissed her again. "I love you, Millie. And I love the inn. I was a stubborn fool about it, but I see now what our life could be if we work together. I don't have much to offer you, but I promise that I'll spend the rest of my life making you happy."

"I think we will be very happy," Amelia said.

"Then I suppose we'd better figure out where we're going to set up house. We can claim the stone kitchen."

"Perfect," Amelia said.

"Compared to the house you grew up in, it isn't much. Just one room."

"Cozy," she said. "How do you know what my parents' house looks like?"

"I thought I might find you there. But I didn't go in. I tried your apartment after the museum, but you weren't there, either. I almost called Edward, but I couldn't remember his last name."

"He showed up at my mother's house. He has a new fiancée. From Argentina. And he's going to help me get my inheritance."

"Then I suppose we ought to celebrate," Sam said.

"Take me to bed, Sam Blackstone. We can drink champagne later."

He grabbed her hand and pulled her along, back to the kitchen. Sarah and James were there, both cutting apples for another pie.

"So is it settled, then?" Sarah asked.

"I suppose it is," Amelia said. "I'm going to be staying."

Sarah gave a little shout of approval, then gathered Amelia in her arms and hugged her. "I knew it. I knew you two belonged together. And now I'll have a sister to help me plan my wedding."

"And I'll have a sister, too," Amelia said.

Sam gathered enough food and drink from the fridge to last a few days and then nodded at his sister and James. "You are officially in command of the inn. We'll see you…when we see you."

"Are we going to be gone that long?" Amelia asked.

Sam nodded.

"Then we're going to need another pie."

Sarah held out a freshly baked Dutch apple. "Please, have this one."

They set out through the snow to the old stone house, the cold making Amelia's cheeks redden. This was what it was like to be alive and in love, she mused.

She'd waited so long for this feeling, and now that it was here, she wanted to make it last. And with Sam Blackstone at her side, she had no doubt that it would.

* * * * *

REQUEST YOUR FREE BOOKS!
2 FREE NOVELS PLUS 2 FREE GIFTS!

HARLEQUIN®

Blaze

red-hot reads!

YES! Please send me 2 FREE Harlequin® Blaze® novels and my 2 FREE gifts (gifts are worth about $10). After receiving them, if I don't wish to receive any more books, I can return the shipping statement marked "cancel." If I don't cancel, I will receive 4 brand-new novels every month and be billed just $4.74 per book in the U.S. or $5.21 per book in Canada. That's a savings of at least 14% off the cover price. It's quite a bargain. Shipping and handling is just 50¢ per book in the U.S. and 75¢ per book in Canada.* I understand that accepting the 2 free books and gifts places me under no obligation to buy anything. I can always return a shipment and cancel at any time. Even if I never buy another book, the two free books and gifts are mine to keep forever.

150/350 HDN GH2D

Name	(PLEASE PRINT)
Address	Apt. #
City	State/Prov.	Zip/Postal Code

Signature (if under 18, a parent or guardian must sign)

Mail to the **Reader Service:**
IN U.S.A.: P.O. Box 1867, Buffalo, NY 14240-1867
IN CANADA: P.O. Box 609, Fort Erie, Ontario L2A 5X3

Want to try two free books from another line?
Call 1-800-873-8635 or visit www.ReaderService.com.

* Terms and prices subject to change without notice. Prices do not include applicable taxes. Sales tax applicable in N.Y. Canadian residents will be charged applicable taxes. Offer not valid in Quebec. This offer is limited to one order per household. Not valid for current subscribers to Harlequin Blaze books. All orders subject to credit approval. Credit or debit balances in a customer's account(s) may be offset by any other outstanding balance owed by or to the customer. Please allow 4 to 6 weeks for delivery. Offer available while quantities last.

Your Privacy—The Reader Service is committed to protecting your privacy. Our Privacy Policy is available online at www.ReaderService.com or upon request from the Reader Service.

We make a portion of our mailing list available to reputable third parties that offer products we believe may interest you. If you prefer that we not exchange your name with third parties, or if you wish to clarify or modify your communication preferences, please visit us at www.ReaderService.com/consumerschoice or write to us at Reader Service Preference Service, P.O. Box 9062, Buffalo, NY 14240-9062. Include your complete name and address.

HB15

SPECIAL EXCERPT FROM

HARLEQUIN

Blaze

*Enjoy this sneak peek at ONE BLAZING NIGHT
by bestselling author* **Jo Leigh**,
in the **THREE WICKED NIGHTS** *miniseries from
Harlequin Blaze!*

Is Matt just a friend? Or a friend…with benefits? Find out!

Samantha O'Connel grabbed her phone. "What?"

"Huh. That's one way to answer the phone."

It couldn't be—

Matthew Wilkinson. Matt? *Matt!*

Sam hadn't heard his voice in a very long time.

Her eyes shut tight as the world stopped turning. As the memories piled one on top of another. He was her first love. And her first heartbreak.

"Hello? Still there?"

"Hu…hi, Matt?"

"How are you, Sammy?" he asked, his voice dipping lower in a way that made her melt.

No one called her Sammy. It made her blush. "I'm… fine. I'm good. Better."

"Better? Was something wrong?"

"No. I meant to say richer."

He laughed. "I'd kind of figured that after reading about your work."

Her face was so hot she was sure she was going to burst into flames. She was a jumble of emotions. "How are you?" she asked instead.

"I'm good. Jet-lagged. Just in from Tokyo."

"Godzilla stirring up trouble again?"

"I wish," he said, his voice the same. Exactly the same.

She wanted to curl up under the covers and dream about him. "Nothing but boring contracts to negotiate."

"But you still like being a lawyer?"

"Some days are better than others."

"And you're living in New York?"

"I am," he said, the words delivering both disappointment and relief. If he'd moved back to Boston, she would've died. "I heard from Logan last night. He said that crazy apartment of yours is not to be missed."

Hi there, worst nightmare! She held a groan. "We haven't talked since you…"

"That's true," he said smoothly. Then he sighed. "I've thought about you. Especially when I've caught yet another article about something you've invented."

She smiled and some of her parts relaxed. Not her heart, though. That was still doing cartwheels. "I'm still me," she said.

"Look, I'm coming to Boston for a few days, and I'd love to stay in that smart apartment. But mostly, I want to see you."

See her? Why? "Um," she said, because she couldn't think straight and this was Matt. "When are you coming?"

"In three days."

No. The word she was looking for was *no*. She couldn't see him. Not in a million years. It would be a disaster. "Yeah. I've got some deadline things, but, you know."

He laughed. Quietly. Fondly. And that was what made him so dangerous. He was rich, gorgeous and could have any woman on the planet. The problem was that she'd fallen in love with him two minutes after midnight on her birthday.

"I'm excited to see you, Sammy…"

Don't miss ONE BLAZING NIGHT by Jo Leigh,
available April 2016 wherever
Harlequin® Blaze® books and ebooks are sold.